BEST
WOMEN'S
EROTICA
2013

BEST
WOMEN'S
EROTICA
2013

Edited by

VIOLET BLUE

CLEIS
PRESS

Published in the United States by Cleis Press, Inc., 2246 Sixth Street, Berkeley, California 94710.

Printed in the United States.
Cover design: Scott Idleman/Blink
Cover photograph: Paul Viant/Getty Images
Text design: Frank Wiedemann
First Edition.
10 9 8 7 6 5 4 3 2 1

Trade paper ISBN: 978-1-57344-898-7
E-book ISBN: 978-1-57344-914-4

"Night School," by Valerie Alexander, first appeared in *Suite Encounters* (Cleis Press, 2012); "Being His Bitch," by Janine Ashbless, first appeared in *Bound By Lust* (Cleis Press, 2012); "Blush," by Mary Borsellino, first appeared in *Going Down* (Cleis Press, 2012); "Exposing Calvin," by Rachel Kramer Bussel, first appeared in *Irresistible* (Cleis Press, 2012); "The Spanking Salon," by Elizabeth Coldwell, first appeared in *Cheeky Spanking Stories* (Cleis Press, 2012); "Susanna," by Krissy Kneen, first appeared in *Triptych: An Erotic Adventure* (Text Publishing Australia, 2012); "Air-Conditioning. Color TV. Live Mermaids.," by Anna Meadows, first appeared in *Suite Encounters* (Cleis Press, 2012); "Normal," by Charlotte Stein, first appeared in *Anything For You* (Cleis Press, 2012); "Last Call," by Alison Tyler, first appeared in *Morning, Noon and Night* (Cleis Press, 2012).

CONTENTS

vii   Introduction: Such Great Heights

1   Salamander • ELIANI TORRES
5   Exposing Calvin • RACHEL KRAMER BUSSEL
15   The Tow Job • JENNY LYN
28   Stop 'N Buy • MIMI KESSEL
42   Normal • CHARLOTTE STEIN
53   Road Crew Cock • SERAFINE LAVEAUX
62   Blush • MARY BORSELLINO
68   The Spanking Salon • ELIZABETH COLDWELL
82   On the Verge • ROSALIA ZIZZO
92   Susanna • KRISSY KNEEN
102   Meet Me at the Spanish Steps • LUCY FELTHOUSE
111   Director Lady • ANIKA RAY
116   Being His Bitch • JANINE ASHBLESS
131   Last Call • ALISON TYLER
142   Highly Inspired • ALYSSA TURNER
154   Air-Conditioning. Color TV. Live Mermaids. •
       ANNA MEADOWS
162   Night School • VALERIE ALEXANDER
174   The Fattening Room • GISELLE RENARDE

185   About the Authors
189   About the Editor

INTRODUCTION:
SUCH GREAT HEIGHTS

This book is a sex toy.

Each story draws a map from where you're sitting right now, straight along the shortest path, to arousal. Like me, you'll read these stories and encounter familiar landmarks set like furniture within your sexual psyche—but in the hands of these supremely talented authors, they don't look quite like you've always remembered them.

> With a one-track mind, Josie ponders human anatomy and what kinky things to do with that anatomy as she sees the players' balls and bats. She likes to feel the balls of her men slapping her pussy lips repeatedly like last week in the library, bending over the table.
>
> But today she wants something a little different.
>
> She wants to feel the hard equipment push into her backside while she bends over, pushing backward, and she wants the guys to enter her in a tight, juicy hole a little higher than they're used to. She wants to bend as if in prayer, as if she were offering her body,

*and for the guys to give her absolution because sex is
her religion.*

—Rosalia Zizzo, "On the Verge"

I took a hard look at the world and business of erotic writing
before I started work on this collection of stories. The genre
is experiencing seismic shifts. Erotica collections are a dime a
dozen these days, and explicit novels of lowered quality become
bestsellers. Women want good porn, but many people still think
that's scandalously breaking news—and continue to sell us soft-
serve when we want hard candy.

*When he handed her the ice-cream bowl, she purred
like Eartha Kitt, "I eat ice cream, you eat me?"*
*"That's the idea," Jeremy replied before diving
at her left thigh. The caramel spread across her flesh
was heavy and sweet, and he licked it like an animal,
working his way up for chocolate from her belly and
marshmallow from her breast.*

—Giselle Renarde, "The Fattening Room"

The stories in *Best Women's Erotica 2013* are designed to do
three things: turn you on, show you sex with the lights on and
transport you into a scene so expertly crafted that you'll revisit
it like a hot porn loop in your head long after the book is closed.
Each of these scenes holds a promise of delightfully nasty replays
for a quick turn-on—just as sure as I can promise you'll wonder
how long you've had your thighs clenched as you page to the
next story, eager to consume the next riveting fuck.

*He can be smooth when he wants to be. Charming,
even. Lots of girls liked him, before I got him.*

But lots of girls probably wouldn't understand him saying—smoothly, of course—"Would it be such a bad idea if we played that game again?"
—Charlotte Stein, "Normal"

Making this edition of *Best Women's Erotica* live up to these promises was no easy feat. But it was the necessary outcome of the problem I was faced with after the last edition was released. Modern erotic writing is struggling for its next Anaïs Nin, its Pauline Réage, its A. N. Roquelaure (Anne Rice), its Emmanuelle Arsan. Looking around at the turbulent landscape of erotic writing in a time when, more than ever before, the most popular erotica was also the most disappointing, it was clear that erotic fiction was having an identity crisis.

...I followed him inside, through to a room with black walls and bare wooden floorboards, lit only by the light of flickering candles in wrought-iron holders. Masked men in formal wear stood round in twos and threes, chatting and sipping champagne.

It struck me this place resembled nothing so much as a miniature version of the gentleman's clubs where discreet networking took place and business deals were struck. A haven where no women intruded and who you knew was more important than what you knew.
—Elizabeth Coldwell, "The Spanking Salon"

To become the promise I describe in the first two paragraphs of this introduction, *Best Women's Erotica* had to demonstrate what the popular new erotic books can't quite seem to grasp: that so-called "women's erotica" is really about superlative writing and believable characters who have hardcore, explicit sex at the dizzying heights of exquisite fantasy *with the lights on*, and you, the reader, get to see *everything*.

I decided that to find the very best stories of the year, stories that were about women living out their unflinchingly explicit sex fantasies (and not overwrought stories starring stereotypes), I had to go about finding stories differently than had ever been done for any edition of the series.

> *I'm thinking about Aurora, about her pressing her ass against him, about her whispering in his ear.*
>
> *"I'd want her to suck your cock while I lick her pussy," I say, suddenly grateful for the cool air, for the fact that I can close my eyes and hear all the city sounds roaring around me and not think quite as much about how that idea makes me blush, makes me shake, makes me—who thought I was so sophisticated and blasé about strippers—tingle as his fingers slide inside me.*
>
> —Rachel Kramer Bussel, "Exposing Calvin"

Rather than putting up a call for submissions for five months and reading through the hundreds of stories that came in, I did this—and much more. Knowing that a number of high-quality erotic anthologies had come out in the beginning of the year, and more were set for release at the end of the year, I reached out to erotica editors around the world.

I asked the writers at the top of the genre—of all the stories they'd read through and selected as the finest for their collections, which stories had they read that they thought were the best? Which stories were the most memorable, and who was the hottest erotic writer they'd worked with?

Now he stood behind Amanda, just as she had done, resting his cock in the crease. He worked the mazes of her ears with his tongue—had a hand caressing her face and lips, another for her breasts—and every so often rocked her suddenly backward, so she could feel him getting harder.

—Eliani Torres, "Salamander"

At the same time I was pestering editrixes far and wide, I looked up erotic authors that were prolific, were favorites online and had loyal fan followings, and whose talent currently cut a swath through the genre. I emailed a selection of these gifted women and asked, which of their stories in the past year did they think were their very best? And, had they read anyone else's erotica that they thought was stunning, arousing?

Say you want a guy to tie you up, and you might win a raised eyebrow. Ask for a spanking, and there's a pussy type of man who will raise his hand—not to smack your ass, but in protest—and tell you he doesn't go in for that sort of thing.

But confess what you really desire, what keeps you up in the night, is to have a line of men take turns fucking you, and you'll find out who your friends truly are.

—Alison Tyler, "Last Call"

My task was set: to track down as much of this erotica as I could find, to hunt and consume all the recommendations my sources offered. I had my work cut out for me. I read outside the lines of my recommendations, too—once people sent me soon-to-be-published manuscripts, it just made sense for me to read all the stories, in fear of missing something hot.

I read hundreds and hundreds of stories—and I'll bet you didn't know that so much erotica was being produced each year. It is: and I'll bet you also don't know—not just yet—that a hell of a lot of it is excellent. It is.

> *I wanted to picture it; wanted to know how he took off his clothes, if he did it slowly or with a boyish smile, or if his clients preferred to unwrap him like a gift.*
>
> *I wanted to know his techniques for pleasing clients; if he was better at being forcefully passionate or tender and sensitive. I wanted to know if he preferred men or women.*
>
> *I wanted to know what it would be like if I hired him.*
>
> —Valerie Alexander, "Night School"

What you hold in your hands is a distillation of all this. Hot scenarios by cream-of-the-crop writers, literary porn that doesn't fade out when the sex starts. Instead, each tale is fast-acting aphrodisiac.

I hope you use this book like the sex toy that it is.

Violet Blue
San Francisco

SALAMANDER

Eliani Torres

She had hoped the sex would be bad. It would serve her right. The blond man Amanda brought home from the park shrugged when she told him she was horny, nothing more—a kind of forgiveness. His name was Sal, like her first high school boyfriend, Salvador Acosta, a church kid who was fearless and raunchy but brushed his teeth before and after oral sex, and made her do the same. Hearing the name again reminded Amanda of standing naked with the skinny boy in front of his parents' twin sinks, squeezing toothpaste, gargling cinnamon mouthwash. A marble Saint Theresa had stood on the counter, all patience every time she watched them spitting pink foam into the swirling waters to either side of her.

But the sex was good after all, that first rough fuck in the hallway between bedrooms, loud and embarrassing in her empty house. They were in fuller voice the second time around, exclamations and murmurs, questions and whispers, traveling each other's bodies and responses. She ran her palms over Sal's hair, a vulnerable fuzz of stubble that drew her hands to it like velvet. She put her nose to his scalp, the fold of his neck, her lips to the place where his biceps tucked against his sides, and breathed in his smell: as clean as new laundry, and she could just keep inhaling while he made fists in her hair, she could keep pulling air deeper and fuller into her lungs, caught by the sleek sweet undertone of his skin. He smelled to her like wonder and like trust maybe. So she latched on to his nape with her teeth, groaning, felt him drop his chin to watch her moving hands, which she had snaked around his flanks to the front of him, as though they were his own.

She thought he would come: the first of it slippery along the inside of her wrist. She'd palmed and squeezed, sliding back and forth, his sheath stretching thin on the upstroke, gathering in soft folds on the way down. But instead Sal reached behind abruptly and pulled her before him; he liked lifting or tipping or lowering her into place—adjusting her—and she wanted to be handled. He was slowing them both down, getting her hotter. Amanda was already sinking to her knees, but instead he put her fingers in between her legs for her, and made her keep them there. He stroked a gloss along each of her hip bones.

Now he stood behind Amanda just as she had done, resting his cock in the crease. He worked the mazes of her ears with his tongue—had a hand caressing her face and lips, another for her breasts—and every so often rocked her suddenly backward, so she could feel him getting harder. She stroked her swelling clit, and the moment he yanked at her nipples—tugging them down as far as she could stand it, running his tongue between her shoulder blades—she frothed onto her fingers, saying that she was, she was going to, she was coming. Only when her balance teetered did he turn her around. She was laughing; he was laughing.

Watching her lover suck her fingers clean one and two at a time, Amanda was thinking of the boys who knew her while she was trying not to become the woman she was right now. That first Sal working a furled hand tight inside her; opening herself to Ruben, who even cried once, and then to Otis in college; a summer spent craving the salt of Malik, which she let course down the back of her throat—she remembered they had been sincere. They hadn't known yet not to keep the promises their bodies made. The men who would love her later, she met after she had forgotten what it was to be worshipped by a young thing simply for being one herself. Like this.

She could not believe the beauty in this unfamiliar face, in eyes clearer and kinder than she had expected, in the tremble of his straining arms, and in his subtle vanities—determined to please her, he'd shake his head at himself when he could tell he'd missed something of her—it all made her forget where on their bodies they were touching and where they were not. She could taste all the wants and the delays of her life, with one sharp inhalation, and then another, if he only held her crumpled against him, if he only doubled her knees back against her chest.

She climaxed again beneath his driving jaw, urging him with yeses, closing her eyes tight, and then heard him give one last noisy lick when she had gone quiet, which made her yelp. Sal poised himself over her belly to finally come, holding her right foot in his left hand to push it back in her direction. He let her know he wanted to get a look at the glaze of her cunt, to see its darkened lips stretched. She groaned at the sound of his voice, so hushed and turned on, and opened herself even more, pulling on one knee and plucking at her nipples. He bit his lip at the sight of her, the stroking both faster and tenser, faint sticky sounds in the moments before he lost control. He jetted a few times—saying, *Here it comes*; saying, *Oh, god*; saying, *Oh, fuck baby*—hot on her belly. They swayed apart while their breath returned to them.

Sal dragged a knuckle across her and painted her chin with it, went back to kissing her, and now his prick squelched in that slickness between their bodies, which melted and tickled her sides where it ran down her ribs. When they peeled apart, she would not look at his eyes, but focused on his chest, those places where his pale hair was gelled by sweat. She wouldn't speak.

He sat quietly with her now, on the edge of her bed, setting his cool foot atop hers affectionately, barely damp. He was curling his toes every few seconds, gently gripping her foot. They faced the brass-edged mirror of her closet a long while, looking at themselves. They didn't assume the luxury of passing out together, interlocked, as she might have wanted, as she wouldn't suggest. A clock ticked on the wooden nightstand, keeping time for her, a slow metronome that would in a few minutes force her to make Sal dress himself and leave.

Amanda's hands were folded in her lap; she still hadn't spoken. Sal had splayed his hands on his knees. She searched his face now, for love or blame, either one of which would have been unbearable. He told her softly that she would be okay. That she already was, didn't she know that? When she nodded wonderingly, Sal shared another burning kiss. The kiss smelled and tasted of her—like wax, like smoke, like the inside of a wineglass—and held promises to herself that she forgot she had made.

EXPOSING CALVIN

Rachel Kramer Bussel

"Let's go to a strip club," I say, my eyes lit up. I haven't been to one in years, and certainly never with my husband. I can see right away from the way he looks at me that he doesn't think we're the type of people who go to strip clubs, all that judgment packed into one lift of his brow, a simple set of his jaw.

"Honey, what? We are not too old. We're forty-two and forty-five? I bet there'll be guys in their seventies there!"

We're on a long weekend in New York City. The kids are with their grandparents. I'm full of energy and excitement and want to do something we can't, or at least, don't, do at home. Plus I want to show him something that used to be a part of my life. No, I was never a stripper, but I used to go to places like that with my girlfriends, just for fun. Calvin's been once, and he said he felt dirty about it.

"Marnie, I just don't know. I don't want to be the guy with his tongue hanging out looking like an idiot because a woman is taking her clothes off. I don't want them to laugh at me. Plus, I have you," he tells me, walking toward me and pulling me close for a hug.

My Calvin is a good man, a good husband, and still hot to me. He was never drop-dead gorgeous but he is sexy in his own way, with his big, slightly balding head, his big hands, nose, body. He's six foot four and husky, whereas I'm a foot shorter and petite. Even when he's not trying to slam me against the wall, a nudge from him in that direction and I'm wet as can be. I'm usually the sexual instigator, and I don't mind. I have a higher sex drive than he does, but he's never turned me down. I've been the one to introduce toys, to get him to relax enough to let me play with his ass while I blow him, to ask him to spank me. It's not that Calvin's repressed, but there is still a part of him that thinks that other people will care what we do in bed, that feels like someone—not necessarily G-d, but someone—is watching every time we do anything the least bit risqué.

That makes me laugh because I'm not an exhibitionist, either, save for my occasional low-cut dresses, and if I thought someone was watching me get it on, I'd be self-conscious, too. We both grew up in small towns with Jewish families that were on the more buttoned-up side, but I escaped at eighteen and never looked back. Calvin, I'm afraid, is always on the verge of looking back, and in our thirteen years of marriage, my job has been to pull him forward, into both the future and the knowledge that he is an adult and can enjoy his body.

Sometimes I do things just to shake him up, like when I went on my last business trip and gave him a bottle of lube and a porn DVD that I'd originally intended to take with me. "I think she's hot," I said, pointing to Jesse Jane. I knew he'd been tempted to roll his eyes at me—the blonde with the big boobs, really?—but then I pulled him down into our easy chair and started whispering in his ear, relaying the filthiest fantasy I could think of, one that ultimately involved his cock shoved between Jesse Jane's breasts. By the time I took his cock out and started stroking it, he could barely last a minute. I know that inside him lurks the heart and soul of a pervy—a nice, friendly, pervy—guy, and I like to bring him out to play when I can.

"Let's put it this way, sweetie; I'm gonna go to a strip club and get a lap dance. You can either come with me or do whatever it is you want to do." We're staying in Times Square, and there's no lack of entertainment. We have theater tickets for Saturday night, reservations for dinner at Peter Luger's Sunday, and our days are filled with friends and art galleries and walking tours. Tonight I want to do something that is just for the two of us.

"Well, when you put it that way...I just don't want you to feel slighted if I get turned on looking at the women."

"Remember the whole porn incident? Your girlfriend Jesse Jane?" I tease him, making sure he looks me in the eyes. My sweet, sexy husband actually blushes when I say her name. "Oh, you didn't forget her?" I ask as I raise my knee and run it against his dick. I know, and, frankly, he knows, too, that I could've shacked up with my ex-boyfriend Billy, who was much more of a lout than Calvin could ever hope to be. But I didn't want Billy, I wanted Calvin, and I'm not so much trying to change him as bring out the side of him I know exists, because I've seen it, felt it, touched it. I don't want a guy who brags about how many women he's banged (for the record, I'm number three on Calvin's list, whereas my list is considerably longer) or ogles every woman he comes across. This isn't so much about the women in the club, as sharing the aura of a strip club with the man I love. And for the record, I wouldn't have really gone there by myself; where's the fun in that?

"But you can't wear that," I tell him, pointing at his overly fussy shirt and dress pants. It's basically a suit without the jacket. "Put on something more casual."

I strip off my jeans and T-shirt and start rummaging through my suitcase, and while I'm bent over, my thong-clad butt in the air, Calvin comes over and takes a little nip with his teeth. Then his mouth shifts, and he's tonguing my pussy through my underwear. He slides them aside and I somehow reach for a little clingy black dress while he goes down on me. I don't say a word because I don't want to break the spell, but soon my thong is around my knees and my husband is kneeling on the floor going to town. He is so good at getting me off like this, and I know that he'd happily stay here all night. I rub against him, press myself down, take everything he's offering. His tongue plunges inside me, pressing upward, then toward the back, before moving on to my clit, but he makes sure to add two fingers. I've taken up to four of his fingers, but two is the magic number. The combination of his fingers and mouth make me go wild, and I clutch the wall with my right hand for support as my pussy tightens, bearing down on him as he finds my G-spot along with the most sensitive part of my clit. He twists and presses his fingers deep inside me while his tongue works its magic and soon I'm shuddering, stamping my foot on the ground, coming hard.

Only when he's ridden out my orgasm with me does he ease the thong off of me then gently pick out another thong and help me step into it followed by an orange silk wrap dress I love because it feels like it's stroking me all over and makes me know I won't fade away against the myriad of beautiful women we're about to see. Calvin likes the dress because it's so light, it's easy to lift it up, or undo the sash holding it together, and get to whatever part of me he's most hungry for. He stands up and doesn't say anything but I can see on his face that the unexpected bliss we just shared was just as powerful for him as it was for me. Calvin's the kind of guy who lives for giving head; any time I want him to do something around the house, all I have to do is promise him my pussy to feast on and he moves immediately into action.

I'm quiet as I finish getting dressed, adding earrings, a little mascara, black eyeliner, and gloss. It's a tricky thing, getting dressed to go to a strip club. You don't want to look like you're trying too hard, like you want to outshine the true stars of the evening. Calvin is quiet, too, and I'm not sure if I've pushed him too far, but I hope not. I am wet at the thought of seeing him surrounded by beautiful women. I don't know why, exactly, especially when many wives would be up in arms at the prospect of their husbands even setting foot in such a place. But I'm cut from a different, naughtier kind of cloth. I think the prospect of seeing a gorgeous woman—glittering, preening, perfect, really— giving her all to making my husband hard, horny and happy, is the perfect way to spend an evening in the Big Apple.

We set out the door, holding hands in the elevator. I overhear another couple talking about the fancy dinner they're about to share and stare at the man, wondering if he'd rather be joining us on our little naked adventure. I've done a little research and found a club that doesn't serve alcohol, which means the women are totally nude. I would've been happy with sexy G-strings but I want to give my man a real treat, want to see him struggle between the side of him that thinks this is somehow improper and the side that would love nothing more than to take a trip to the champagne room with a woman who's built for sex, or at least, is selling us on that image.

We walk to the club, and I smile at the man checking us in as I give him our IDs. He leads us to two chairs that have a view of the stage, but are separated from the other patrons a little. Almost immediately, a svelte woman with black bangs and hair that slithers down her back greets us. "Hello," she says, beaming at both of us. "Can I get you a drink, or perhaps a bottle?" I've set aside cash for tonight, because I don't want that to be an issue.

"A bottle of Veuve Clicquot," I say, and she smiles and walks away briskly.

"You planned this?" Calvin asks, looking a little stunned.

"Maybe," I tell him. "Why, do you have an objection? Is it a hardship to be surrounded by so many hot women?"

"No, not at all." I can tell he wants to tack on something more, but I put my finger to his lips.

"So then enjoy it. I plan to." With that, I tug him down into his seat. He just stares at me, then at the woman who approaches us. She's short and petite, the opposite of my five nine and major curves. I can tell immediately that he likes her.

"Hello," I say to her. "I think my husband would like a dance. This is Calvin, and I'm Marnie."

The girl giggles, then says, "I'm Aurora, and I'd love to give you a dance. Is it for both of you?"

Calvin is about to nod when I shake my head. "I want him to get the dance, but I'll watch. Maybe I'll get my own after. I don't really like to share," I say, letting my eyes do the talking.

She winks at me, then walks over and whispers something into Calvin's ear before rumpling his hair. She takes off his glasses and even before the next song is officially on, she is starting to put the moves on my man. His head is thrust into her cleavage and I turn just enough to fully absorb what's happening. I see him slowly start to surrender—to her, and to me, to the idea that it's okay to want her, okay to get hard, okay to succumb to the beauty all around us. And it is beauty, even though I know so much of it is artifice. I don't mind, because I can separate the two, and focus on just the former.

I can admire Aurora's ass covered in just a glinting gold thong, her feet raised on five-inch black and gold shoes, her nipples so perky as she rubs them right up against my husband's cheek. I have a feeling she probably wouldn't be quite so touchy if I wasn't here, but maybe she really does like him, or just wants a good tip. I don't really care, because the sight is making me want to touch myself. When the song officially starts and she bends over, thrusting her tits out to the club while her round ass, small yet firm, backs up against my husband, I put my index finger in my mouth, bent at the knuckle, needing somewhere for my oral fixation to land.

Suddenly I almost wish we'd hired a woman who'd do more than Aurora would, because I'm aching to suck her nipples, and to have Calvin know I'm sucking her nipples. He looks over at me and seeing me with my finger in my mouth makes him shudder. Then a new fantasy washes over me: I want to be the one giving Calvin a lap dance, right here, right now. I want the eyes of envious men staring over at us; strip clubs seem to be the land of the grass always being greener.

I like that aspect of what we're doing as much as anything; I want people to know we're together, to know that I'm not just putting up with my husband getting a sexy dance from a crazy-hot chick, but that I'm loving every minute, that I'm paying for it. I reach for his hand and when our fingers touch, the spark is electric. I smile at him and he seems to let out a silent groan, almost overcome with delight at what Aurora is doing.

The song can't be more than four minutes long, but it seems to last for ten. When she's done, she whispers something else to him, kisses his cheek then comes over to me. I hand her her fee, then slip an extra twenty down her G-string. "He's a lucky man," she whispers in my ear, filling me with her sweet, special scent. She stays poised at my ear for a few seconds longer than she needs to, and it's my turn to shudder. Truth be told, I'd love to feel her rub her body up against me, but not here, not now, not with all the men ready to circle like vultures, to turn something admittedly wanton but also a little bit sensual into mere masturbation fodder. Plus I want, more than anything, to talk to Calvin, to hear from him exactly what it was like.

"Next time," I whisper in her ear and I'm treated to a kiss on my cheek, too, and a brush of my lips across her breasts, a whisper of what I'm giving up. Yes, I know she works on tips, but there is something unmistakable about the way this woman moves, and either she's the best actress in the world or she's as bisexual as I am, the kind of woman who tends to go for guys until a woman comes along and makes her head spin.

She smiles and, holding hands again, Calvin and I watch her sashay across the room. The look on his face when I turn to him reminds me of when he wakes up from a wet dream, like he can't quite believe what's just happened and wishes, at least a little, it were still happening. "Are you ready to go?" I ask him.

"We can go to a club back home, too, sometime."

He just looks at me for a moment, then stands, pulls me up and gives me one of the most passionate kisses we've ever shared. This is big, for him: to grab my ass and shove his tongue in my mouth and press his hips right up against mine in public like that. I love knowing that people are looking at us, that they see how much we want each other. As we walk out, I let my curiosity bubble over. "What did she whisper to you?"

"How badly do you want to know?" Calvin asks, and it's my turn to swat his ass.

"Just tell me! This was my idea, I think I deserve to know."

"Okay, okay, don't get bent out of shape. Or do…" he says suggestively, moving to bend me as much as he can while we're out on the street. "She said that she hopes I lick your pussy really good tonight, that she hopes I show you a good time in exchange for buying me the dance. Actually, she made me promise I'd lick your pussy until you came."

"I wonder if she's thinking about you with your head between my legs right now," I whisper in his ear as we waited for a light. "I hope so. I think that'd be hot. I think it'd be hot if she watched us, if she were right there in the room while you licked me."

My normally mild-mannered husband then pulls me aside, away from the corner, and backs me up against a brick wall. His hand goes to my ass and starts massaging it, and I can feel his hardness pressing against me. "Tell me more, Marnie. Tell me what you want Aurora to do." Then he somehow positions his body so he's blocking me from view of the busiest street we're near and slides his hand along the slit of the silk dress, then up, up, up, until he's at my panties. Anyone walking by on the other side would probably notice something odd, but I don't mind. I'm thinking about Aurora, about her pressing her ass against him, about her whispering in his ear.

"I'd want her to suck your cock while I lick her pussy," I say, suddenly grateful for the cool air, for the fact that I can close my eyes and hear all the city sounds roaring around me and not think quite as much about how that idea makes me blush, makes me shake, makes me—who thought I was so sophisticated and blasé about strippers—tingle as his fingers slide inside me. The power has shifted from me to him, and Calvin knows it as he works his digits deep into me, pressing softly but in exactly the right spot, his thumb caressing my clit.

"I can hear her sucking you, swallowing you, and feel how wet it's making her. I love knowing she's getting so turned on by your big dick." I have to stop talking because what he's doing to me is just too much. Well, not so much that I want him to stop, but too much to enjoy while I'm talking. Calvin's lips swoop in to kiss me while he fucks me harder. I think he might be trying to say something into my mouth but I'm not really sure, I just know that I feel Aurora's spirit here with us as Calvin makes me come with his fingers, trapping me against the wall so I don't fall down.

Finally, he's done, and he pulls his hand out and lets my dress fall back down while I rush to retie it. "You were right, Marn. We're not too old at all. Now come on, don't dawdle. I have a promise to Aurora to keep."

When we get to the hotel, Calvin strips me naked and positions me so my ass is flush with the window, which faces another hotel's windows and is probably visible from several office buildings. There he gets down on his knees and eats me to three more orgasms, only letting me taste my fill of him when I assure him that I'm more than satisfied, for the moment, anyway.

It turns out exposure goes both ways, and I'm more than ready to bare myself to millions of strangers if it means discovering a new side to the man I thought I knew better than anyone. I may have to go back and thank Aurora before we leave. I think she deserves to know that Calvin is very much a man of his word.

THE TOW JOB

Jenny Lyn

The temperature outside the car was dropping toward the low thirties and a light drizzle had begun to coat the windshield. A late fall storm was coming. I wondered if I might even see a few snow flurries—just as the Porsche's engine began to sputter.

"He's going to be so mad," I said to the steering wheel.

After typing out a short text, my thumb hovered over the SEND button on my phone while I worked up the courage it took to press it. He could be out with friends having a good time, or at home, tucked in his warm bed asleep. It was a Friday, and I was probably one of the few fools who chose to work late on Friday nights. What if he said no? What would I do then?

He'd warned me the last time, and I'd made him a promise that I hadn't kept. Now I was going to be in trouble for that transgression. I shivered as the cold from outside began to seep inside the car, and reached into the minuscule backseat for my sweater. If I didn't do something soon I was going to freeze to death right here, in the barren parking lot of a dilapidated shopping mall five miles from home. No heater, no radio, not even a bottle of water. Thank god I at least had cell service.

I sent the text and waited.

His response came within seconds. *Remember what I told you the last time?*

Yes, I replied, because, dammit, I couldn't say no. He'd made me repeat it back to him twice just so we were clear.

Give me the address.

I could practically read the aggravation in his succinct order; see the severe expression on his face as he'd typed the words.

I did the best I could and tossed my phone in my purse then thought better of it and held it in my hand in case I had to call 911 before he came to my rescue. Finding me stranded in a rather desolate part of town was just another reason he was going to be pissed.

It couldn't have been more than fifteen minutes, though it felt like an hour, before bright headlights flashed through the interior of the car and Sam backed his giant tow truck up to the front bumper.

The driver-side door opened and he dropped to the ground, all two hundred and fifty pounds of rock-solid male, dressed in weathered jeans, a black T-shirt and scuffed shit-kickers. I knew what kind of power that impressive frame held. Suddenly I didn't feel as cold anymore. Sam was just so...there, so big and intimidating and mean looking, especially now as he glared through the front windshield of my car and signaled for me to pop the hood.

Through the gap under the open hood I watched his hands move deftly from spot to spot as he checked over the engine, my body tightening with anticipation and nervousness. This situation was quite similar to the way this thing between Sam and me began, except that time I hadn't made it out of the parking lot at work. He'd towed my car back to his shop then given me a lift home. We'd sat in my drive and talked for two hours. When I went back to pick my car up two days later, we'd had sex in his office. Twice. That had been four weeks ago. Since then Sam had become intimately familiar with the inner workings of both my car and me. He was adept at making my motor purr, the car... not so much. And if Sam couldn't fix it, it couldn't be fixed.

He finally slammed the hood and the expression on his face was grim, like he'd seen something akin to a crime scene under there, a dead body with its throat cut. Not a chance in hell of saving it. All we'd been doing for the last few weeks was prolonging the inevitable with patch jobs, pouring money into a bottomless hole. "It's terminal," he'd told me. "It'll cost more to fix it than it's worth."

He stalked around to my door, snatching it open. I shrunk back in the seat as he leaned in.

"Grab your stuff," he said sharply, "and go wait in the truck where it's warm."

Yep, he was angry. I nodded, scooping up my purse and leather portfolio. He did take my hand to help me out of the car, but he let go as soon as I stood.

While I waited in the heated cab of Sam's truck he went about the business of readying my poor car to be towed under a steady drizzle. He climbed back inside and tossed his gloves behind the seat before passing a palm across his wet, closely cropped black hair. I watched appreciatively as the muscle in his bicep bunched before he dropped his hand to the gearshift.

"Sam, I—"

Stormy blue eyes flicked to my face. "Save it, Jane."

Shit. I didn't like a mad Sam. A mad Sam was worse than an aggravated Sam. I'd seen that version the last time this happened, the night I'd made that promise. I faced forward, rubbing sticky palms down my skirt, and buckled my seat belt for the ride back to his shop. The short, quiet trip ended with us pulling through one of the massive bays in his garage.

Sam's company was one of only a few in town that worked on foreign cars, and he was obviously successful at it. The garage was state of the art, fairly clean and roomy, and the tow truck we'd ridden in still carried that faint new-leather scent.

Still, all I could smell was Sam, the soap on his skin mixed with a trace of rain. He didn't smell like he'd been out at a bar with friends; he smelled like he had just showered, probably ready for a cold beer and some couch time after a hard day at work. And here I'd gone and interrupted that with my neediness.

He never asked me out for a Friday night because he knew my weeknights required as much downtime as his. I wanted the same things when I got home—a hot soak and some peace and quiet. Honestly, though, if he did ask I would say yes, no matter how exhausted I was.

Right now I wanted to see Sam's anger abate, to taste him on my tongue, feel his heat against me, his hands manipulating my body any way he chose to do so. He was very good with his hands, but then why wouldn't he be? They were what helped make him his living.

Mostly, I wanted to know that I hadn't pushed him past the point of caring about me and what happened to my stupid, worthless car.

I watched out of the corner of my eye as he shoved the gearshift into PARK, unbuckled his seat belt and dropped his hands to his thick thighs. When he sighed I looked over, waiting for him to say something.

He stared through the front windshield. "You broke your promise, Jane."

"But—"

Another stern look shut me up. "I don't want to hear an excuse. You promised me the last time this happened that you'd look for something else to drive. Doesn't have to be new, even though you can certainly afford it, just reliable. Am I wrong?"

"No."

"And what did I say would happen if you broke your promise?"

I closed my eyes, remembering what had been happening to me when I made him that promise. He'd tied me to the bed facedown, my arms stretched above my head, while he'd fucked me roughly from behind. I'd carried bruises on my hips from his fingertips for the past week. Not that I was complaining. Every time I looked in the mirror I reveled in those marks, his marks, beneath my skin, the memory of that night turning me on all over again. Every single time.

I swallowed hard. "You said there'd be consequences."

"Take off your panties."

My gaze flew to his face but it was a blank slate. "Sam."

"Do it now, Jane, or call someone to come pick you up."

Well, I didn't want that. I wanted whatever I had coming to me, or so I thought. I unbuckled my seat belt and reached under my skirt, sliding my underwear off and handing the scrap of black lace to him. He tossed them on the dash and slid to the middle of the seat.

"Now the sweater and blouse."

My fingers shook as I did as he asked. He draped them over the back of the seat then patted his lap.

"On your stomach."

Oh, holy hell, this was going to be painful. But didn't I deserve it? Hadn't I let him down? It shouldn't matter to me. We weren't necessarily a couple, though deep down inside I admitted that I wanted to be. He hadn't expressed a desire for more than what we casually had. At least not yet. But it did matter. I hated that sound of disappointment in his voice, hated to see it buried in his eyes when he looked at me. He was the first person in a very long time that I could count on unequivocally, that I wanted to get close to. I wasn't about to let that slip through my fingers, not when I might be able to fix it.

I kicked off my heels and slowly crawled across his lap, dropping my hips down onto his thighs. My knees were slightly bent, bare toes resting on the cold window. I stretched my arms straight out, gripping the edge of the seat near the driver's door.

One large, restraining hand twisted in my hair, pressing lightly against the back of my neck while the other coasted up the back of my thigh, pushing my skirt up with it. Everything inside me seized with tension. I bit my lip and waited as he bunched my skirt around my waist, exposing my bottom. Heat flared in my face and I pressed it to my biceps. Sam wasn't having any of that, though. A suggestive tug on my hair forced me to turn my head to the side.

"I need to see your face," he explained gruffly.

His palm slid over the curve of one cheek, the roughness of his skin making mine tingle, before the weight of his hand lifted then came back down hard. I hissed at the stinging pain, the fire exploding in my ass. My nails dug so deeply into the leather seat there would probably be permanent indentions left behind. He kept going, delivering slap after slap to my sensitive flesh, spreading the blows from the tops of my thighs up over the curve of my butt.

I'd never gotten a spanking before, not even when I was a child and I'd been very, very bad. Back then I'd just been ignored. I should've known Sam wouldn't let me get away with anything. He'd never given me less than his full attention.

He stopped to rub the burning skin while I tried not to

whimper. I did pant a little. It hurt, but at the same time that delicious heat was spreading through my pelvis, down to the apex of my thighs where I was growing wetter by the second. I squirmed as he firmly kneaded one cheek, and felt his cock swell against my hip. I'd have loved to know what he was thinking, but I didn't dare ask.

"Are you going to keep your promise now?"

I quickly nodded my head, not trusting my voice.

"Say it, Jane."

"I...I promise," I whispered.

He smacked my ass again and I squeaked in protest. Just when I was getting accustomed to the hurt... "You promise what?"

His hand eased down between my thighs, finding my soaked pussy. A low moan escaped my throat as his finger lightly strummed my clit. A teaser. God, did I ever want him to make me come with that long, rough finger. It wouldn't take much. Everything inside me was coiled and ready. I knew what he was offering, but I had to give him what he wanted first.

"Jane?"

The words rushed out. "I promise I'll look for something else to drive."

"When?"

I huffed. "Sam! I can't—"

The hand on the back of my neck tightened in silent warning before he delivered another hard smack to my burning bottom. I nearly came right then. The pain...oh, it was good—a deep hot ache that had spread like a wildfire. Was it wrong that I wanted more? But I also wanted Sam inside me, soothing that ache from within.

"Please, Sam," I breathed.

"Not until you say what I want to hear, sweetheart."

The tender endearment brought tears to my eyes so I squeezed them shut. "Tomorrow. I'll go tomorrow. I promise."

"Much better." His strokes turned gentle then, soothing on my sensitized skin. "You should see your ass right now. It's always been a sight to behold, but it's even prettier when it's bright pink with my handprints all over it."

Oh, yes, I wanted more of his marks on me. The faint bruises and welts from his strong hands, the lingering soreness, all of it a stark reminder of what it felt like to be under Sam's control.

He found my clit again and circled the swollen, slippery bud. My thighs parted a little more, giving him room to manipulate me. I groaned as a potent pleasure flooded every muscle. Ah, yes, just a few more...

He abruptly withdrew his hand and patted my tender bottom. "Up you go."

My head sprung up. "What?"

"You heard me. You didn't think you were going to get off that easy, did you, Jane?"

"I didn't get off at all!" I scrambled to my hands and knees and Sam unzipped my skirt.

"That's the point. Take that off."

I shoved it down my legs, kicking it haphazardly to the floor of the truck. At this point I didn't much care about my clothing, I just wanted Sam to finish this torture and fuck me.

He grabbed my hips and forced me down to straddle his thighs. Then he used the sleeves of my blouse to bind my wrists together behind my back. With barely a flick of his finger the front of my bra popped open and he moved the lace cups aside and out of his way. His thumbs brushed my nipples, making them pucker tightly while we both watched. I craved his mouth, his tongue, his teeth, but I knew I didn't get a say in what happened.

Sam unbuckled his belt, unzipped, and freed his cock. I did whimper then, a needy, desperate sound that should've embarrassed me had I not been so far past that point. He was big and thick and ready, a drop of milky fluid beading on the plump tip. My thighs tightened over his as he sheathed himself in a condom.

Then he was lifting me up and over him, lowering me down one slow, torturous inch at a time until he was seated so deep it almost hurt. The stretch was sublime, the hard press of him inside me forcing my head back and my eyes closed again. Instinctively I wanted to move, raise my hips and impale myself again and again, but his fingers dug in preventing me from doing just that.

Another form of punishment, having to sit completely still with his cock inside me.

"Jane, look at me."

I tipped my head down and opened my eyes.

"Do you understand why I got so angry?"

I heard it then—the frustration and hurt. I bit my lip to stop it from trembling. "I think so."

"Because of exactly what happened tonight. It's bad enough that you work late all the time, but having an unreliable form of transportation is unacceptable."

"I just hate to get rid of it. It has…sentimental value."

"Honey, it was a piece of shit back when your brother drove it. Sentimental or not, it's still a piece of shit. You're the fucking Assistant D.A., for Christ's sake. You live in that tiny one-bedroom apartment with no goddamn furniture. I'm pretty sure you can afford a new Porsche if that's what you want."

I dropped my eyes to his throat. "It's not that I don't want to spend the money, it's just…"

He forced my chin up. "What?"

"I like having you rescue me. If it wasn't for my shitty, hand-me-down car, I would've never met you."

Sam's hands cradled my face. "Oh, baby." He finally, finally, kissed me, long and slow and sweet. His cock pulsed inside me and I squeezed my inner muscles around him. That garnered me a sharp nip on my bottom lip. "I'll still be around to rescue you whenever you think you need rescuing."

"Would now be considered one of those times?"

He popped me on the ass again and I winced. Chances were good I wouldn't be able to sit down tomorrow, at least not comfortably. That was going to make test-driving vehicles rather difficult.

He dropped his mouth to my breast, laving my nipple with his tongue before pulling away with a scrape of his teeth. Banked lust flooded my body like a dam had burst.

"Do I have to beg?" I asked, practically whining.

He smiled, so wicked it should've been illegal. "Tonight, yes, I think you do."

I took a deep breath. It was one thing to think it, yet quite another to say it out loud. "Please, fuck me, Sam."

"No."

I felt my eyes widen in shock. "No?"

"No," he repeated firmly. "If you want it, you're going to have to take it, Jane."

"Oh." Well now, he was being a sadistic bastard, wasn't he? And no doubt enjoying every minute of watching me struggle with how to deal with it. I fidgeted on his lap, testing my range of motion and balance. With my hands tied behind my back, I had nothing to brace myself with, nothing to use for leverage. This would probably be the un-sexiest fuck in the long and storied history of fucking.

Tentatively, I lifted my hips. The slow, sweet drag of Sam's cock inside me was enough to make me forget my awkward-ness, and certainly enough to make me want to continue. I was careful that I didn't go too far. If he slid free of me I wasn't sure he'd be so gracious as to reinsert himself.

How he managed to look so unaffected was beyond me, and more than a little frustrating. His expression remained stoic as he kept his eyes trained on my face. The only telltale sign of his own excitement was the flush of color on his neck and the way his lids dipped over his slightly dilated pupils as I slid back down.

Working my legs farther apart, I shifted more of my weight toward my knees and tipped my shoulders forward. It helped, and I began to slowly ride Sam, letting the pleasure build to where it had been when he first speared me on his rigid cock.

His hands remained lightly clasped around my thighs, his ass planted firmly in the seat. If I was going to get there tonight, it would be of my own doing. But I couldn't give up, could I? Giving up would mean so much more than just forgoing an orgasm. No, this was a test I had to pass. I had to show Sam I wanted him enough to deal with his consequences. In for a penny, in for a pound. If I quit, I might as well delete his number from my phone and forget I ever met him, and I wasn't about to do that.

I was swimming in a thick, swirling haze of sensation. It started inside my pussy and crawled up and out, infusing my body with warm bliss. Everything else fell away but us—Sam and I—cocooned inside the warm cab of his truck with nothing but the heady smell of sex, the wet sounds of me sliding over him, and the unforgiving grip of need. It squeezed me tighter and tighter with every stroke of his cock across hypersensitive tissue. An orgasm built, but would it break? Could I come this way, with no extra stimulation to my clit or breasts?

Sam's face tightened in front of me, the muscle in his jaw

jumping as he clenched his teeth. So yeah, he wasn't that impervious. "I wanted to do this in the truck for a reason, Jane." Whether he knew it or not, his fingertips had started to press into my thighs. I made some noise of pleasurable agreement and he continued. "Now every time I climb in here to go work a job, I'll think of this. I'll remember the sight of your pink ass...how hot it was under my hand."

Yes, keep talking, Sam. Almost there...

"I'll think about how beautiful you looked riding me, your pussy tight and wet and warm around my dick."

Maybe it was the spanking, or his words, or being forced to wait with Sam's rigid cock buried deep inside me. Perhaps it was because I had to work so hard to get there, but whatever helped it along, I came so hard my eyes crossed.

"That's my girl," I heard him murmur softly, his pleased tone breaking something wide open inside of me.

Sam finally relented on his self-imposed, no-help rule; grabbing my hips and lifting me before slamming me back down with a deep, drawn-out groan of completion. My hands were freed and they automatically curled around his neck. He pressed his face to my shoulder as our breathing gradually calmed.

Through the back glass of the truck I watched as tiny specks of white began to drift through the beams from the security lights. It wouldn't last long, probably melt the second it touched the ground. I didn't want to go home to my cold, empty apartment. I'd rather stay with Sam, in his giant bed on sheets that smelled like him, encased by his warmth and strength.

"Can I stay with you tonight?" I asked, afraid that he'd say no. And if he did, it would be more punishment, whether he intended it that way or not. His denying my request would hurt worse than a spanking. I would feel it deeper, in places that had never been hurt before.

His arms tightened around my waist. "Of course you can. I would've asked, but I didn't want you to think I was doing it because I didn't trust you to keep your word about tomorrow."

I pulled back so I could look at him. "I would never think that about you, Sam. It was me who broke that promise, and I deserved what I got. But if you had ignored my text for help, I would've deserved that, too."

"That wasn't going to happen, Jane." He brushed my hair away from my face. "I just needed you to understand where I stood. I'm not going to let you take chances with your safety. You're too important to me."

I smiled hesitantly. "I am?"

"Yes, you are." One corner of his mouth curved into a crooked grin. "Does that scare the fuck out of you?"

I thought back to earlier in the night, when my car had given up, leaving me stranded in that deserted parking lot. I had been anxious then at being somewhere unfamiliar and alone. But it hadn't been near as frightening as the possibility of Sam telling me no, he wasn't coming to my rescue. And it had nothing to do with the car itself and everything to do with the chance that my failure to honor my promise might have caused me to lose him forever. It wouldn't happen again.

"No, it doesn't." I kissed him, whispering against his lips, "I'll never break another promise to you."

"Yes you will." His huff of laughter brushed across my cheek while one calloused hand rubbed my sore bottom. "But that's okay. I know how to make you keep them."

STOP 'N BUY

Mimi Kessel

The first thing I noticed about the Stop 'N Buy near my apartment in Seoul was their reluctance to furnish carry bags, no matter how much you bought. Next was the guy who worked the night shift.

Shops are way too free with bags in the States. I was used to declining them and grabbing my purchases off the counter and stuffing them in my purse and pockets and looking like a maniac. So Korea wasn't any different, except my friends had convinced me that no one in Seoul drinks from the tap. I could see my apartment building from the Stop 'N Buy, and that was the only time it ever occurred to me to buy water. I never left the store with fewer than a couple of two-liter bottles in my arms. I also couldn't seem to learn the Korean numbers, so my transactions and exits were less than graceful.

The first time I passed the store at night I did a triple-take, turned around and walked in. He was leaning over an open textbook on the counter and didn't look up when the doorbells jingled. I pretended to scope out the snacks as I checked him out. He was tall with high cheekbones and refreshingly unfussy hair, which happened to be perfect.

I grabbed a package of something and headed for the wall of coolers. At first I had favored a brand of water that featured a cross section of a volcano on the label. Now I bought Doosan for the sole reason that the bottles were rectangular and easier to stack and grip. I grabbed a few and approached the counter.

He glanced at me once and preformed the rest of the transaction without looking at me. When he told me the total I craned my neck to read the register and I felt a smirk coming off him. As we exchanged money I offered and received with my hands in the traditional gesture of politeness but he didn't bother reciprocating or even saying good-bye. He was reading again before I was gone.

It was everything I couldn't resist: a touch of home, where customer service was extinct if it had ever existed, and a handsome, indifferent man.

I started making all my purchases at night. When I got more familiar with the currency and brushed up on doing addition, our interactions were smoother. He was the least ingratiating man I'd come across in Seoul, a place where I got a more attention than I cared for.

Once I was waiting at the bus stop in front of the store when he arrived for a shift. I was applying a ridiculously expensive shimmery gold-pink lip-gloss that had been a going-away gift. When I received it over farewell cocktails I immediately put some on. One friend nodded with approval and the other said, "That is THE label in Korea. You need to flash that logo whenever you can."

Mr. Stop 'N Buy watched me put on the lip-gloss and I wish I could say that he smiled at me, but he was laughing.

I could see his point. The people all around me were perfectly groomed and tastefully dressed; I was wearing hooker boots and a frumpy parka. I never saw a woman who wasn't perfectly made up and certainly none applying so much as lipstick in public.

He never greeted me when I came in the store. He was usually at the counter studying, but occasionally he was on the floor doing inventory. He wore the store uniform, a sleeveless smock, as if it wasn't there. I thought of his style of dress as spotless grunge, but he stood up too straight and moved too decisively to resemble any hipsters that I knew. It was a dead giveaway that he had already done his service in the army.

Eventually he began to say good-bye in an offhanded manner. It was mechanical and not much fuel for my crush.

One night I set down a miniature carton of milk and other odds and ends that would equal breakfast. He stared at the goods on the counter and gave me a calculated look of mild surprise. I felt my face flush and I hurried to get a couple of bottles of water.

I wondered if the convenience store employees called me "Two-Waters White Girl" or maybe something less kind. I had worked in bars and restaurants for years; in my last stint I had waited on "No Seasoning," "Aquaman" and "The Unfortunate Redhead." But I decided to believe that the ice between us was broken, though I knew I was just completely predictable and constantly underfoot.

When I got back to my apartment I took action, because that's what text translation Internet sites are for. I typed into the void *Come over anytime, have a beer with me. Goldenville, Apartment 607.* Since I had to take the translation on faith, I fastidiously copied the Korean characters onto a piece of notepaper.

The next night I dumped an unusually large pile of goods on his counter. When he got to the two-liter bottle of beer he seemed close to smiling, but it didn't manifest. I was crazy to even think about propositioning someone who had never even smiled at me.

As he rang up the total I taped the folded-up handwritten invite to the beer bottle and pushed it to the side. I paid and began my frantic routine of stowing food and water into my bag and onto my person and I ran out of the store as I said good-bye. I hurried to my apartment and even bolted the door behind me.

I took a long shower, knowing that he was on the clock and there was plenty of time. I also knew that he wasn't coming, which was beside the point. My pussy had been wet since I'd stared the caper, so I decided to cash in. I imagined that he was standing behind me and soaping me up. He spoke softly as his hands slid over my body. I had no idea what he was saying but I could hear amazement in his voice as my breasts filled his hands. One hand stayed with my tits as the other headed south. I could feel him looking over my shoulder at his wandering hands, and his erection pressed into the middle of my back. I closed my eyes and managed to keep up the fantasy that he had pushed his fingers through my neatly trimmed bush and was lightly tracing my pussy from stem to stern. When my fingers found the wetness inside, Mr. Stop 'N Buy became a bystander who was welcome to observe. I thought about his cool manner and imagined him watching me polish my clit to the high burn that I had going. I was sure he would be fascinated, and I slipped a few fingers into my pussy as I came.

Relaxed and clean, I toweled off and continued to prepare for my guest.

I felt virtuous if I wore underwear at all; forget about matching a bra to my panties. Thankfully, a friend of mine had forced a simple black lace set on me, "for emergencies." This clearly qualified, and I slipped them on. It also rated eyeliner and mascara, but I stopped short of full makeup. I would be sleeping in it, which was silly, but I told myself that it would save me five minutes before work. Finally I quit my primping and lay down. I hadn't sleeplessly awaited anyone with that much anticipation since I stopped believing in Santa Claus.

My doorbell rang; it was an endless synthetic chime that could be heard several floors away. I sat straight up in bed and noticed that I was in a T-shirt and sweatpants. Guess I got cold. Guess I fell asleep. I ran to the mirror to check my face. It was passable, and I opened the door.

He stood two feet from the doorway and had to fully extend his arm to present me the bottle of beer I'd left behind. He held his other hand to his mid-torso in the manner in which a Korean man offers things politely.

"Ahn Kyungbin," he said, as he made a self-referential gesture with his hand.

I introduced myself and held the door open wide as I held my breath and waited to see if he would come in. He hesitantly stepped into the tiny entrance area and I tried to entice him farther by offering him a pair of slippers. He shook his head at the slippers but stepped out of his shoes onto the floor. He had removed an article of clothing and my stomach flipped, though I knew that it signified nothing about my chances of getting the rest of his clothes off.

The apartment was one room with a wall of closets and kitchen appliances, a double bed in the opposite corner and a very modest expanse of hardwood floor. The heating unit was inside the floor, which made it inviting and a dust magnet. I was glad I had wiped it down that day because it was the only place to entertain.

He seated himself on the floor and set the canvas bag he was carrying beside him. I placed myself opposite him.

First he brought out the bottle of beer that I had used as bait.

Next was a bottle of *soju* and two paper cups. He opened the *soju* and served me with lowered eyes, one hand held gracefully to his chest. I took the bottle from his hand when my cup was full and filled his glass, minus the grace. I looked into his eyes and let the sounds from the cup tell me when to stop.

We toasted each other. *Geonbae* was one of the seven Korean phrases that I knew.

Then he brought out a package of the sweet corn snacks that I was addicted to. He had been paying attention.

I started to get a dish, but his fingertips touched my forearm and I froze. He proceeded to skillfully open the bag, pulling each seam apart until it was a rectangle of Mylar with a pile of snacks in the middle.

I said the Korean word for *good* or *cold*—they both sounded the same to me.

The picnic started in earnest. He laid out shrimp puffs, dried squid, chocolate-dipped pretzels, chocolates with liqueur centers and an assortment of neatly packaged cakes that I had never ventured to try. He rounded it out with a couple of *onigiri,* triangular-shaped portions of rice wrapped in sheets of seaweed, which he must have known that I practically lived on. When I reached for an unopened treat he looked at me and shook his head slightly. He had everything opened as neatly as the first bag in a few minutes. When he began to drink his *soju,* I helped myself to the squid.

There weren't any words to take the edge off the tension or to gauge my chances. Not knowing what would happen next, much less anything about him, kept me in the moment. I felt his every move and could smell a scent on him that I didn't recognize. It was a cross between wood shavings and clover and something I couldn't place.

I wondered if I had the ability to seduce a man without

speaking to him. I wasn't bad looking and my body was slamming, but I thought that I had always talked myself into the best lays. The Korean phrase book that I carried around actually had the translation for, *I think I am ready to be intimate with you.* Would I have to place my finger under that phrase and smile winningly to get fucked?

We had eaten almost everything and killed the bottle of *soju.* I got some glasses and the bottle of beer that I'd put in my tiny, empty fridge. We served each other with less decorum than before, but courtesy was the only language we had in common.

As soon as I set my glass down after our second toast he touched the hem of my T-shirt. He rubbed it between his thumb and forefinger and looked at me. I gave him an unambiguous smile and he helped me out of it.

I felt more at ease in just the bra; the oversized T-shirt was all wrong. Since I was up against a language barrier signals were everything. I unbuttoned his shirt and drew the sleeves from his arms. His chest was developed and defined without being bulky, just as I'd imagined earlier in the shower. He stood and pulled me up by my hands. I got busy unbuttoning his pants. It struck me that I hadn't undressed a man in years; if my partner wasn't already naked, I would ask him to strip. As soon as I got his jeans over his hips he yanked my sweatpants to my ankles in one motion and got rid of his jeans as efficiently.

He knelt on the floor and slid the remains of the picnic to one side with his forearm. He pulled me down to my knees and we kissed.

It's one thing to discover how someone kisses; it's another thing to learn almost everything you know about somebody through kissing. So far I had deduced that he was extremely confident but I couldn't have predicted the sensuality that went along with his self-assurance.

Apparently the banquet was just beginning.

His hands and mouth were busy and leisurely at the same time. Wherever they went they lingered in small, subtle activities. I felt his hand move under my bra and free one of my breasts. He tucked the length of his thumb into the fold beneath my breast and I felt the weight of my tit pressing on it as the rest of his fingers cupped the flesh passively. He tugged the bra back into place and ran a finger along the edge where the lace gave way to skin.

At the same time he was taking the measure of my lips, rolling my bottom lip between his and sucking it into his mouth before his tongue sidled up to mine.

As he reached the other side of my décolleté he rolled the fabric down over the nipple, leaving it exposed. It was hard and erect and the other seemed close to pushing a hole into the flimsy lace. He was polydexterous; as he toyed with my bare nipple his tongue roamed my mouth. It felt so good that I caught myself wondering why it hadn't been in there before. He pushed my hair away from my face. As we kissed he continued to stroke my hair until he gently pushed me on my back, his hand cradling my head as it met the floor.

He stacked his body on top of mine. I could feel each of my bones being pressed against the wood floor. Sandwiched between the warmth of his body and the heat of the floor I felt completely consumed. His tongue filled my mouth and I ran my hands over his backside. His flexed triceps told me that I wasn't bearing the full brunt of his weight. His powerful shoulders led to back muscles I wasn't even aware existed. As my hands skimmed his back I brought them to each side of his waist. The feel of his taut skin over layers of muscle was intoxicating. His body was perfect, not least his ass. What started as gentle stroking turned into a pry-it-from-my-cold-dead-hands grip, and I fought against the temptation to have a go at his asshole.

He pressed up on his arms, and I instantly dropped my hands to the floor.

He made a gesture like he was putting on ChapStick. I was puzzled until he pointed to my purse and I remembered the lip-gloss encounter.

I fished it out of my bag and handed it to him. He withdrew the brush from the tube and sniffed it. To me it smelled of cotton candy, apricots and lilac. I don't know what it smelled like to him, but he seemed pleased.

He knelt next to me and leaned in. He brought the brush to my mouth and carefully outlined my bottom lip. It wasn't necessary, but he refilled the brush and painted in the rest of it with short, precise strokes that evenly spread the juicy slick.

He paused. Just in time I stopped myself from automatically doubling my lips.

He closed the lip-gloss and admired his work. He slipped off his briefs and sat back. He was fully erect and I was completely turned on.

He leaned forward and kissed me, carefully avoiding my sticky lip. As he pressed his mouth to my cheek he slipped his arms around me and undid my bra. He took it with him as he sat back on his haunches.

"Pretty," he said. I guess he'd been saving that one up and the surprise and the approval were thrilling.

He reached for the lip-gloss again and I held very still, after I had pushed my tits out slightly. Carefully he painted my top lip as thickly as he had the bottom. He grasped the waistband of my panties on either side of my hips. I lay back and lifted my ass and he pulled them off.

He hiked my knees up and spread my legs and took a good look. I propped myself up on my forearms and watched him, and I saw his hand groping for the lip-gloss.

You've got to be kidding, I thought. I knew where he was headed. That and his soft exhales on my pussy were killing me. He began painting my labia with small, delicate strokes and frequent dipping. The two flaps of skin clung together but he attended to them separately, gradually coating them in a clockwise direction. He hadn't gotten far when I felt my pussy open. He took his time and eventually the rim surrounding my cunt was as shellacked as my lips.

I know that my nipples and my clit are hardwired—if one was getting attention I felt it in the other—but this was a new one. I was licking and rolling my lips long before he laid a tongue on my pussy.

He sat back again and looked at the big picture. I could feel my own juices oozing over the lip-gloss, and I wondered if he could see anything for the glare. I lay back and imagined his view and anticipated his mouth on me.

He leaned back in and tortured me with more forceful breathing on my swollen pussy. Then I felt the tip of his tongue dip into the stickiness for a moment and withdraw. I knew that he was tasting the slickness and I wondered if he could distinguish my taste from the lip-gloss's. His tongue took another swipe at the sparkling ring of honey, and I imagined it dissolving in his mouth as he savored it. At last he began to lavish my pussy with little licks. At first I was overwhelmed by the sensation. When I pulled myself together I could feel that he was methodically distributing the lip-gloss with small flicks of his tongue, first outward and then inward, barely sinking his tongue into my cunt.

The gloss was evenly spread and it had begun to set up—my entire pussy was coated in a hard candy shell that was dripping with my own juice.

His lightened the pressure of his tongue and just slipped it around in the nectar. He completely ignored my clit and slowly circled the mouth of my pussy in one direction. My own tongue mirrored his movements on my lips. Both openings were unbelievably sensitive. He had made the connection, but I knew what it called for.

Sixty-nine is fun, but I've never thought of it as a main course. Someone was usually being neglected and I took giving and receiving head too seriously to do it half assed. But clearly the only thing that would satisfy me was my over-lubed lips on his cock as he sucked at my gloss-stiff pussy.

I sat up, and he watched to see what came next. His thick lips were a solid shimmer of golden-pink. He was a pretty boy and he would make a fiercely beautiful woman. I pointed to my lips and then to his and laughed. I finally got a little smile out of him. I gently pushed him on his back and climbed on top. As I looked into his eyes and idly wondered what was going on behind them I softly placed my lips on his. They stuck together on contact. I pulled back just a fraction and the bond was tested but held. I lifted my head, and the seal broke with a quiet smack. I turned away, scissoring my arms and legs until we were tops and tails and I was staring at his cock.

His dick was perfect for my purposes, beautifully shaped and totally rigid. It was just a bit too large for me to swallow completely, but I knew I could suck him properly without using my hands. I felt his breath on my pussy again and I guessed that he was waiting for me to make the first move. I was glad because I was going to take pleasure in giving him the blow job of my life, and hoped that he would enjoy it too.

I lightly pressed my mouth to the tip of his cock. I had barely parted my lips and I suddenly found my mouth full; the lip-gloss had removed all friction. It was an oddly familiar sensation that

I didn't connect with giving head. I gently held him in my mouth for a moment. When I tightened my mouth around his dick I realized that this was what it felt like to be fucked—except I was in complete control.

I was dying to feel the effortless glide of my lips over his cock again. I released suction and raced up and down his shaft. I had never enjoyed taking a cock in my mouth so much or thought about the pleasure of the man on the other end of it so little. His hands were moving over my hips and ass but I was more aware of my cunt empathizing with the comings and goings in my mouth.

My pussy contracted. I tightened my lips and forced them over his cock, making his engorged flesh shift to either side. As I released his dick from my lips on the way back up I felt his hands lower my hips and place my pussy on his mouth. I bore down on him again with tightly pursed lips and as I squeezed over the plump head of his cock I felt his tongue enter my pussy. As I gradually took his cock into my mouth his tongue ventured deeper.

I jerked my head up and his tongue withdrew. It could have been coincidence—one way to find out. I touched my lips to the tip of his dick and he pressed the flat of his tongue to my pussy. As I took the head of his cock into my mouth he barely entered my cunt. As I gently popped it in and out of my mouth his tongue matched my movements perfectly. He would be my mirror. I took in more of his length and his tongue shot into my cunt. It was so exciting that I nearly came immediately.

The sweet smell of the lip-gloss mixed with the even more delicious smell of sex. I had this naughty feeling that I couldn't explain; I was no stranger to receiving oral. As I tested his ability to mimic my attentions to his cock I understood where the hint of taboo was coming from—I had never gone down on myself before. That almost made me come right then, but I told myself to cool it and that was the last conscious thought I had.

I swirled my tongue around the tip of his cock until I couldn't stand the resulting sensations in my snatch. I switched to meandering figure eights that staved off another near orgasm. My pussy was on the edge of becoming too sensitive, so I thrust his cock into my mouth. I sucked him off slowly, swallowing as much of him as I could without effort.

I was rewarded with the tongue fuck of my dreams. He kept my unhurried pace, and the way he slipped his tongue in and out was almost nonchalant. I increased the pressure on his cock and I instantly felt his tongue unfurl inside me and his thrusts became crisper and gained speed. I caught up to his rhythm and maintained it.

He held my ass tighter and was mostly able to keep me from bucking and grinding. I didn't mean to interfere with his work, but I couldn't help myself. I couldn't deny myself any longer either.

I swallowed the entire length of his cock, straining to get it all in my mouth, confident that he would return the favor. I tasted a bit of precome as I clamped down and sucked him hard.

He was equally merciless. He drove his tongue deep into my cunt over and over, waggling it as my tongue circled his cock. I started to come. He must have felt my initial spasms, but if he had any doubt the way that I went all out on his cock made it plain. We fucked through my orgasm and I almost lost my mind. It was within my power to make him slow down or even stop, but I was going for broke. As my orgasm wound down and the nerve endings in my legs and feet lit up, I felt his dick contract slightly. He was ready to go. He continued to mirror my every move, but I turned my full attention to his cock. I closed one hand around it, determined to make it up to the inch at the base that had been somewhat neglected. I only got a few full strokes in before he exploded in my mouth. I worked him until I felt his tongue motionless inside me. I stopped moving but held him tight.

When he softened I rolled off of him, but I didn't have the will or muscle coordination to go far. I woke up as he was removing my thigh from his neck. He helped me into the twin bed and I lay in his arms.

I pretended to sleep. I was completely relaxed but I knew from the semi-daylight coming through the window that it would be time for work soon.

We were both sticky all over from the lip-gloss and my ample fluids. I slipped out of bed and ran a wet washcloth over the worst of it in the bathroom. If anything, I figured the lip-gloss scent overpowered the smell of sex. I did have smoky eye makeup going and maybe more bed head than was appropriate for the office. I got dressed quietly, but the closing click of the wardrobe door woke him and he sat up.

I said, "Work," and gently pressed him back down. On an impulse I picked up the lip-gloss. It was hot from lying on the warm floor. I slapped some on, distributed it with a wink of my lips and dropped it. I gave him a deep, sloppy kiss and left.

All day long I prayed he would be in my apartment when I got back. He wasn't. There was no sign of the picnic, the glasses were put away clean, the bed was made and the lip-gloss was gone.

NORMAL

Charlotte Stein

I guess we look like any normal couple. More normal than any normal couple, in fact. He wears plaid shirts and khakis, and I wear twinsets, and we go to town meetings. While at the town meetings, we eat the normal amount of free cookies and sandwiches and sometimes we have punch. Everybody shakes our hands and no one averts his gaze, so I know we at least seem ordinary.

But I know they'd think something different if they were with me in the entryway to our little normal house with its painted shutters and the welcome mat at the door. Normal couples don't do what we're doing, with the autumn air still rushing in from outside and his hand just reaching to put the keys on their hook.

That's right. We have a key hook and winter jackets and a doorbell that chimes the theme from "The Simpsons." We also have a game where I put two fingers to the back of his neck and say, "If you move a muscle, I'll blow your fucking head off."

He doesn't move a muscle. We've played this game often

enough for him to know not to. His hand hovers near the hook, as still as if some gunman had really come up behind him and pressed the barrel to his skin, but more impressive than that is his other arm, the one that's slightly curled because he was also going to take off his jacket and now he's caught. It must be uncomfortable, being frozen in that half-caught-in-a-sleeve position, but he manages it. He always manages it.

One time I snuck up on him as he was bending over to run a bath, and he stayed like that, too. Hunched, barely balanced on anything stable, one hand reaching, just like now. And he'd remained that way for as long as I required him to—though when you think about it, what sort of person would refuse to with a gun pushed into the small of his back?

It's these little things that make me certain he believes the act, utterly. He believes it in a weird way, as though some part of his brain is always just waiting for this and inside that part, he's sure: *I would freeze in position until my muscles burned and my head swam, if this really happened.*

Though the word *this* has a little leeway in it, because I know what he does if he's actually threatened. One time some guy tried to grab my purse and he yanked him back by his jacket and punched him in the face. Really quick, too, as though he didn't have to think about it and the guy should just get punched. He's a big man, so it's not as though he has anything to be afraid of.

But he's afraid of this, because this isn't some guy mugging us in a parking lot. *This* is something else altogether, something weird that started for reasons undisclosed. I want to say it started because we were messing around with water pistols and somehow I pinned him down, though that word somehow has a lot of leeway in it, too. It bends as far as *he kind of let me* and *I kind of liked it,* and then I said, "I'll smack you with the butt of this thing if you don't stop your fucking squirming," and he looked…I don't know. The way he sometimes looks when I go down on him.

It's very easy to tell, on him. It's how we ended up going out in the first place. I was shy and he was too cute, and I didn't realize he wanted me until I gave him a friendly hug and saw his flushed face afterward. I rarely know when a man is progressing toward turned on, but it had been pretty obvious, then. He gets all hot eyed and fidgety, and the things he says aren't as smooth as the things he was saying before.

He can be smooth when he wants to be. Charming, even. Lots of girls liked him, before I got him. But lots of girls probably wouldn't understand him saying—smoothly, of course—"Would it be such a bad idea if we played that game again? You know. The one with the water pistols."

Though of course we don't need water pistols, now. My fingers are enough, like little kids playing cops and robbers, only he's the cop and I'm the robber and I always somehow get one up on him. Even when it's just my fingers. Even though he's a foot taller than me and built so big it sometimes makes me shiver just looking at him.

I'm wet already, and I don't know if it's because of him and the way he smells tonight—like that good aftershave he bought—or because of the game. The game. The one that's probably taking over our lives.

I mean, we play it at least once a month, now. That's bad, right? Or is it just bad that we play it at all? Normal couples play games, I know it. But they don't sound like our games—or maybe they do.

Just the other way around.

"Please don't hurt me," he says, and I wonder who he imagines I am. Is that what this fantasy's about? Him imagining me as someone else, someone rougher—maybe even a man?

Just because he reacted differently when it really was a man—
that doesn't mean anything. That was reality. This is fantasy.
It's different, when you can control all the parameters. It's
different when you know someone might really hurt you or hurt
your wife.

It could be that he secretly wishes I was big and strong and
masculine.

Though when I really think about it...the things he's actually asked for...the ones he's dared to voice despite the fact that
neither of us really discuss this...they were all very one way.
You don't ask someone to push her breasts into your back when
you want to pretend it's a man attacking you. And somehow I
doubt you'd need someone's pussy all over your face, if you were
desperately craving dick.

But even so these little doubts linger in my mind, until I'm not
really sure what I'm thinking anymore. I just do it, instead, and
that's much better. I tell him to move forward into our house and
not to make any sudden moves, and he obeys me exactly in these
little, tentative, shuffling steps.

Just like the real thing. Though I'm not sure how I know what
the real thing is like. Or why I enjoy this, if I let myself think
of things like that—how scared and full of hesitation someone
would be, with a real gun to the back of his head. How his mind
would race with everything some pervert could do.

Only I'm the pervert. Once we're safe inside, I tell him to start
taking off his clothes, and there's really nothing more you can say
about that. It's weird and wrong and my body hums with it until
I think I might pass out. My clit is a swollen heartbeat between
my legs and my nipples are diamond hard, and when I hear the
jangle of his belt and the rasp of his zipper, everything gets worse.
Or better, depending on your point of view.

I wonder if it's the wrongness that makes it sweeter. That

vague idea that this is *his* weird fantasy, but *I'm* the one getting some illicit, bizarre sort of pleasure out of it. Does he know I do? I can't see how he could fail to. Whenever we get to the good part I'm always as wet as rain, and I come hard. I come with barely a hand or a mouth on me—I can just slide down his cock and that's it, right there.

I suppose it's the power dynamic. The shift. Something like that. But when he's stripped from the waist down and I can see the strong shape of his good thighs and the almost-tender curve of his ass, I'm not so certain anymore.

I want to bite that ass. I want to scratch it. I want to leave perfect red streaks all over his pale, unblemished skin, so that he's just a mixture of white and red and black. And that seems even more wrong than the thrill I get, the pleasure of putting two fingers to the back of his neck. I mean, I love my husband. I love him truly, madly, deeply. There's no urge in me to hurt him, not really. We've never so much as exchanged brutal words, the way some couples do. Just the thought of seeing his face fall as I say something rotten makes me curdle inside.

The rotten things don't ever even occur to me, because he's a wonderful man. He doesn't leave his socks out; he's never late. He supports me in everything I do and it feels like something natural to lean into him when I'm in need or feeling blue.

And yet here we are.

"Is that enough?" he asks, but he already knows the answer. No, the pants are not enough.

"All off, bitch," I say, and though the word feels kind of silly in my mouth he shivers on hearing it. Shivers, and obeys. I step back and he pulls his shirt over his head, then the T-shirt underneath.

It feels kind of weird to keep the pretense of a gun up, clasping one hand over the other and poking one little finger out, but I do it anyway. Because that's as much a part of the game as his acquiescence. The feel of that fakery against my palm makes me strong and like a different person, until I can feel my shaking legs growing stiff and firm and my aching body aches harder, hotter.

"What are you going to do to me?" he asks, which only makes me think of the things I've done before. All of them make my face heat. Once, I made him masturbate while I took pictures—I have no idea why. These things just come to me like the next bead on a rosary I'm fumbling through, and I never quite know what it's going to look like until it's there in front of me.

"I haven't decided yet," I say, and he moans. It excites me, that moan—because I recognize it so intimately. It's the same one he lets out when I'm pushing up against him or maybe rubbing him through his pants, and he knows, he just knows that soon we'll be making love.

But then he says, "Please don't hurt me," as a little chaser to the too-excited sound, and then I'm all mixed up and inside out again. A little kick of heat goes through me and I tell him to shut his fucking mouth. I tell him I'll hurt him if I want to, and nothing he does will stop me.

He's panting now. Harsh and rattling, like he's trying to get it under control.

"You feel so safe in your neat little world, don't you," I say. I'm not asking.

"I…" he starts, but doesn't finish.

"Until right now, I bet," I tell him, then press my two fingers to the naked small of his back. When that doesn't provoke a strong enough response, I run them down his spine, over and over. I wait, until he tries to squirm away from me.

And then I get a fistful of his hair and yank his head back.

He makes a little sound low down in his throat, which lets me know the move has shocked him. And my teeth suddenly in the soft flesh close to his shoulder, the tauter flesh over the round bone—that shocks him, too.

But I can tell he likes it at the same time. I know for a fact that he loves having his hair pulled and he always goes limp when I bite him, though it's neither of those things that confirms how arousing he finds it. It's the shock and his reaction to it. His sudden wateriness, like his knees have turned to jelly.

He likes it best when I'm unexpected. As though this could be real, it could all be real, and there are no limits to my brutality.

I think it's this idea that pushes me farther. Like he's goading me into more, and I give it. I grasp his fat, stiff cock just as he's getting his bearings from the bite and the hair pull, and I squeeze hard.

Though it isn't the feel of me that makes him moan and gasp, I know. It's what I say; it's the words that force their way out of me—they're the ones to blame.

"Oh, I see," I tell him, and I barely have to say anything more. My tone is so cruel, so cruel—god, I never imagined I could be capable of this much cruelty. I sound like the curving, sharp edge of something nastily mocking, and his moan melts down into embarrassment. Mortification, in fact.

"One of *those,* huh?" I ask, and he tries to curl away from the press of my palm. The squeeze and release I get up to, with my teasing, torturing hand. It always amazes me, at this point, how I manage to manipulate a body so much bigger than mine—how I can twist him back against me and get my hand around him and whisper in his ear. Though secretly I suppose I know he's helping me. I can feel him putting his weight on the balls of his feet. Holding himself, for me.

Is it weird, if that turns me on more than any pretense at reality?

"No, I'm not, I'm not," he says, which only makes me wonder

what he thinks I mean. What *those* am I talking about? What kind of weirdo does he think my mind is conjuring up?

"Your body doesn't lie," I say, and I feel so sick, so wrong, I'm such a bad person.

Until he moans and pushes into my hand, and then I don't know what I am.

"Get down on there, you little slut," I say, then watch as he does. He even does it in just the way I'd imagined—crouched on his knees on the couch, elbows on the arm so he's kind of on all fours.

Though I don't know why I imagined that. I've gone past the fumbling and into some kind of insane autopilot, and it's like someone else is telling him to reach into the drawer next to him and get out the baby oil that I don't want to think about why we keep there.

We keep it there in case our elbows get dry, right? A dry elbow emergency in the middle of watching "The Wire." Right?

Somehow, I don't think dry elbows make a person breathe as hard as he's doing. Or shake as much as he's doing. And from here I can see the slant of his gorgeous face, and it's flushed and weird and any second he's probably going to come all over the couch.

I think I want him to. No, I definitely want him to.

"Now make yourself nice and wet for me," I say, though my insides balk at the words and I'm halfway certain he won't understand what I mean. It's too filthy. He'll never get it.

But then he says "Okay, okay, just don't hurt me," far too quickly. And he doesn't beg, even though most of the time he at least puts up a little resistance. This time, he slicks up his fingers—just two of them, as though he's done it many, many times before—and slides them between the cheeks of his perfect ass.

As though he's done that before, too.

Though he struggles, when it comes to the thing I didn't even know I wanted. Or he wanted. And I can see he's never really done this before, at least—penetrated himself with two fumbling fingers. His body's long and it's a hard reach, and when he turns a little I can see the mixture of emotions on his face. How they've fought until they've made his expression slack. He can't hold them all together.

He doesn't know what he's doing, and it's then I know. I have to help him.

"Move," I tell him, as though he's just a nuisance. He's in the way and I'm going to show him how it's done, even though I've got no idea.

Lucky, really, that it's so easy. I just kneel behind him and stroke between the cheeks of his ass until he stops jerking or trying to jolt away from me, and then real sudden he spreads open beneath just ever so slight a pressure, and I'm sinking one finger all the way in.

Of course, it's gentler than a real attacker would be. But he still begs and says "No no no," and tightens around that intruding thing, to the point where I'm sure I should stop. He doesn't like it. This isn't what he wants. It's hot and amazing and the weirdest thing I've ever done, but he doesn't want it.

So I go to pull away. I think of some bullshit thing I can say that will keep us in the game but let him off the hook, like, *Knew you couldn't take it*—but that's the moment he chooses to push back against my hand. The way I do, when he's got me on all fours and he's just teasing me with his cock, just promising to thrust in hard and fast until I'm sobbing.

I think he sobs, too.

"You like that, huh? Look at you, taking it. Whore," I say, because I'm bad but he's worse. He tells me "Ohhhhh, yes I am,

I am, I'm such a whore," and pushes and pushes back against the finger I'm fucking him with as though he can hardly contain himself.

I can't concentrate on how it feels—silky, I'll probably think later, and vise tight—or whether it means he really does want a man to fuck him. Maybe, though I don't think wanting to experience something in your ass is quite the same as wanting some hairy big-thighed fucker doing you—but I can concentrate on how it feels for *me*. I'm too hot inside my clothes and I've soaked through my panties, while the urge to rub myself against the curve of his ass grows immense, impossible.

I need to come. I think he needs to, too. He's babbling things that are not words and every now and then I catch him trying to push his swollen cock against the silk of the couch. I tell him I'm going to fuck him, now, and he tries harder, moans louder, his eyes barely seeing me when I force him to turn over.

I slide my finger from his ass and he rocks back and forth as though feeling the absence too strongly, but when I push my little fake gun into the soft place just below his jaw, he goes still— the kind of still that suggests a trembling tension, just below the surface.

"Don't you fucking move while I do this," I say, but he's too far gone to stop himself making noise. Or jerking upward as I wriggle out of my panties and get myself over him.

"Please," he says, though I can't tell if he means *please do* or *please don't*. He just stares up at me with his dark, too intense eyes and waits for me to slide my embarrassingly slick pussy down over his tensely hard cock.

It feels like bursting. He feels much too big, and I'm much too worked up, and I can hardly do the thing I usually do—fuck him hard and fast and brutal, as though I'm sticking something in him rather than taking something in.

So to compensate, I get a fistful of his hair. I clench it tight between my fingers and call him a slut, a dirty slut who just loves getting fucked by anyone, anyhow. I think of lurid porn movies and a million men saying *You want every hole filled, don't you, whore?* and it comes easier, then. I tell him he wants something in his ass and something in his mouth and something around his cock, and though I'm sure it should sound silly, it doesn't, somehow.

It sounds dirty and hot and nasty as fuck, and even more so when he pants "Yeah, yeah, I want to be used, I want to be used up."

I think it's that word—*used*. I think about how many times I've felt that way in my life, just because someone did something he could never bear to. And then I come hard, in great breaking swells, with his cock still jerking inside me and my hand still in his hair and not a thing touching my clit.

He can do that. And it makes it better when he follows almost immediately after, hands suddenly on my thighs as his hips snap upward, uncontrollably. I can feel him coming thick and strong, and it's good enough that he can't seem to make any sound. His mouth just makes one big O and his eyes go back, and I know, I know, I understand.

What he needs—it's not the same as what's normal or good or right. It's something different and strong, and it guides like a hand on the back. Like a gun at the nape of his neck. And that's okay, because it guides me, too. I'm bleak and blank with it.

And even if they could see how normal we're not, I'd do it anyway. I would, I swear I would. The gun is at the nape of my neck, and I can't do anything but.

ROAD CREW COCK

Serafine Laveaux

Traffic is snarled up the entire way home, leaving me with nothing to do but stare at the highway department crew as they scurry about the new lane under construction. At a quarter of a mile per hour, I have plenty of time to study them.

Sweaty men, mostly in their twenties and thirties with a few that look fresh out of high school. They have on too much safety gear to see much but I imagine them shirtless anyway, sleek muscles rippling from collarbone to cock, dripping with sweat.

The image has my pussy dripping as well. It's been nearly six months since I've gotten laid.

One of them catches me watching and favors me with a wave and a grin. I wave back, then lean my head back against the headrest and lower my hand to my lap, hiking my skirt up. Without taking my eyes off of him, I began to stroke my lips and clit through the thin fabric of my panties, imaging it's his fingers doing the walking. I picture myself getting out of the truck and bending over the tailgate, ass bared and cunt flared, a wide-open invitation for him to come and get me. Imagine the faces of shocked commuters as they see my flushed pussy exposed for the highway crew; what a nasty, dirty slut they would think me, and I like it. I slip a finger under the elastic, dipping it between the satiny folds just beginning to lube up, then slide it up to my rising clit.

The worker I'm eyeballing keeps glancing over at me, finally stopping his work and nudging one of the others, pointing at me. *Do you see that filthy bitch,* I imagine one asking the other. *I bet she's got her fingers in her cunt right out here in public.* Ha! The taller one is grinning like maybe he does know what my fingers are sliding into, the second guy smiling but confused. I pause my clit massage long enough to raise my fingers where they can see them. They're slick with cunt juice, and the two men are close enough I know they can see that. Tall guy's eyes widen as I pop my fingers in my mouth and suck them clean, just as the taillights in front go off and I let off the brake.

"Holy SHIT did she—" but his voice is lost as traffic briefly surges forward another twenty yards. And then stops.

"Fuck." Not that I love being stuck in traffic, but I would have liked to have tortured them a little while longer. Returning my fingers to my eager cunt, I look for another worker but the rest of them are too busy working to notice me.

Two hours later, after the grocery store, the dry cleaners, the hardware store and the bank, I'm finally heading home. As I pass the spot where the crew had been earlier, my heart speeds up in anticipation, but for nothing. It's past five, they're already gone and traffic is moving too fast anyway.

My exit is about five miles out of town, leading to a far-to-market road that leads to my house another ten miles off the interstate. Going home to an empty house, my wet pussy frustrated at the prospect of another night of shower-spray love, I nearly miss seeing an older model Chevy truck pulled off to the side of the road and up on a jack stand. One tire is lying in the grass beside it, and two men are pulling a tire out of the bed. As I glance back in the rearview to see one standing in the road staring at me, I'm floored to see it's the highway crewman I'd watched earlier. As I turn onto the road to home, I steal a glance to the right and see both men are now watching me drive away.

The voice inside my cunt speaks up.

Go back.

Bullshit, I can't. That's crazy.

Pussy. You know you want to, and what's the harm? It's not like they know you.

As logic and lust argue, my hands take over and swing the truck in a wide U-turn back toward the crewmen. Even as I draw up to the turn, I tell myself this is fucked up, I can't do this.

My heart is racing and my cunt throbbing. Logic tries one last time to talk me into turning around, and then my fingers revist my cunt. God, it's still flooded from earlier, and I know I'm going to go for it. A thousand no's resound in my head but I ignore them, rolling through the four-way stop and heading for the unknown.

My truck roars up the wrong way on the exit, and as I pass the two guys the taller one drops the tire behind the pickup and leans against the truck, assessing my arrival. I U-turn again and pull over into the grass behind them. For a moment I sit frozen. The blood rings in my ears; nothing has ever turned me on like this. Is this what drugs feel like? If so, how does anyone ever stop?

My mind shuts down, pissed that I'm completely ignoring it. Vaguely I realize I've turned the ignition off and gotten out. The two are motionless, silent, as I approach, but their eyes give away their shock. They say nothing, and that's good because if they do I will likely race back to my truck and haul ass away. In the wake of their silence, I walk between them to the back of their truck. Lowering the tailgate with shaking hands, I step up onto the tire left on the ground, one foot on either side, and then bend over.

Looking over my shoulder at them, I put on what hopefully looks like a seductive smile, then reach back with one hand to pull the hem of my skirt up a notch. They look at each other, and for a moment I'm afraid they'll try to be gentlemen, think maybe I've been in the sun too much. *Shit shit shit.*

The taller one is the first to shake off the shock and step up to the plate of ass being presented to him. Lifting my skirt to my hips, he strokes, then squeezes my ass with both hands. His hands are rough and strong, and I picture his thick, calloused fingers pushing into my cunt. I hear a gasp; maybe it is me.

"Unreal," someone says in a shaking, barely audible voice. A hand slides underneath me to grasp first one tit, then the other, fingers lightly pulling on hard nipples as they go. Another group of fingers trail their way down the crack of my ass until they reach my cunt, where they begin to explore every millimeter with excruciating slowness. Sliding between my lips, his finger and thumb grasp my clit and begin to rub the tip in a circular motion. I'm starting to writhe with pleasure, the joy of having hands not my own finally on me, and as his finger begins to flick my clit I feel like my cunt is expanding, opening up wide, inviting him to slip something more than a puny finger inside.

God, it feels like I could fuck a cannon right now. A car honks overhead, and I realize people passing by on the overpass can see us and I'm glad. I want them to see me, hope they see these strange guys with their fingers and cocks all over and in me, imagine them pulling over to jack off while watching me, thinking what a fucking beautiful nasty slut I am and oh, god, wishing they could fuck me too. Fuck, I need more.

Another hand squeezes my left asscheek. The second guy has decided to join in.

"Goddamn look how wet she is!" and he's not kidding. I feel my slick juices running down the inside of my thigh, and there's a cock grinding against my thigh, marinating itself in them.

"Put that fucking thing in me," I beg, then I feel tall guy's cock pushing through my swollen lips and plunging deep into my aching cunt.

"Oh, fuck, yeah!" I cry out, back arched, head thrown back. "Fuck that pussy," I order him, and he complies with enthusiasm, his hands grasping my hips, keeping me supported as he hammers into me.

Second guy has his cock out, stroking it roughly. He reaches out to grab my hair and tugs my head toward him. I haven't given head in a long time, never really enjoyed it, but suddenly I want nothing more than a dick in my mouth. I turn my face toward his thick, brown cock and open my mouth willingly. He takes my head in both hands and pushes his cock deep into my mouth. My eyes close, the smell of cock and balls filling my head. I'm stuffed on both ends, people passing by see me taking it from two men and I see myself from the passing cars: thin brunette with her skirt thrown over her back, bent over, one man face-fucking her and another fucking her from behind. I want them to see me now, and tonight when they go to bed, and think, *Why couldn't I fuck that bitch too?* Right now I could fuck them all.

"Take it all, bitch," second guy orders and I do fuck, I gobble his fat cock to the root and even try to suck his balls in with it. *Bitch, dirty little bitch, yeah, I am,* I think, or did I say that out loud? How can I when I have at least eight inches of thrusting cock in my frantic mouth?

Tall guy's hands pump me on his cock, balls slapping at my clit with every stroke. *Slap. Slap. Slap,* and with each slap I feel a small ripple run through my belly in response. Second guy's hands in my hair as he pumps my head as well, and I release all control as two men I've never seen fuck me like a rag doll, thrusting and pumping and yanking and shoving me. My mouth is connected to my pussy with cock, full of heat and wet and even pain but oh, fuck, I want more and those ripples are rising faster. Through my stuffed mouth I'm moaning and begging, *Fuck harder you fuckers, fuck harder,* and they do.

Fat cock thrusts into my face, balls slapping my chin, and I feel him begin to shudder, and he's coming. He starts to pull back, but I grab his shaft with one hand and won't let him. Sucking and licking, swallowing his cock as I shove it in this time, and then a hot salty load shoots down my throat and second guy calls out something in Spanish. Instinctively I suck greedily, suck every last drop from his softening cock, come dripping from the corners of my mouth. He finally pulls away, but I'm not ready to let go just yet. "No," I beg. "I want you."

"Jesus Christ" he rasps, hanging on to the side of the truck.

"Fucking god, I'm so goddamned horny!"

Suddenly I feel tall guy's cock pull out. "NO!" I cry, but he's not leaving me just yet.

"Easy honey, I'm just changin' gears. Givin' that pussy a rest."

He moves to my front and presents his cunt-slicked cock to me. The damn thing is a beast, rising nearly to his belly button. It's nowhere near as thick as second guy's, but it's considerably longer. I lick my lips and he grins. "That's right girl, you're gonna suck that cock clean now." He grasps my head and begins to face-fuck me, his fucking yardstick of a dick choking me with every thrust. I start to panic, it's so fucking long there's no way.

"Relax, don't fight it," he orders, and I try to follow the advice, relaxing my head into his hands and letting my throat go slack. "Good girl," he says, as the massive shaft keeps coming in, until I'm about to gag again. "Now swallow," he says, and I do, and his cock slides into my throat. I swallow again, and it must feel good because he gasps. Relaxing is the key, fuck, it's the key to it all. I'm free from expectation, released from performing. All I need to do is relax and get fucked and fucked and fucked. Relax and let the cocks and fingers and honking cars fill my mind and body and as they do the ripples start up again and I follow them.

Without warning, my pussy is stretched wide as second guy, apparently having recovered his hard-on, slams inside me. He's not polite about it, and his engorged cock feels twice as large in my cunt as it did in my mouth. My body is rocking back and forth with the combined pumping of the two men. I envision myself hanging in space, suspended on two cocks that meet in my core, as the ripples become waves that surge through me. My eyes are closed but the black somehow spins behind my lids.

Oh, god, oh, goddamn fuck goddamn, I scream soundlessly and the two cocks keep pumping in and out, forcing me to the top of the waves as my cunt begins to convulse in ecstasy. Heart explodes, lungs heave, my arms collapse beneath me only to be yanked up by someone. My eyes blind, a roaring in my ears, excited grunts behind me, clit promising a fucking tsunami on the horizon with every gentle slap of second guy's balls and suddenly my cunt clamps down on his cock like a pit bull as I come harder than I've ever come before. Screams erupt—I've never screamed during sex but I am now, screaming through ten inches of dick that does little to muffle me.

For a moment I'm spent, satiated, and my body sags against

the tailgate. Tall guy's cock pulls away, but this time I'm too blissed to beg it to come back. Dimly I hear second guy coming, and I feel it shooting over my pussy, heat on top of heat.

"Dammit, Angel, whyja do that, I wasn't finished back there."

Angel, second guy's name is Angel, he of the husky cock.

"I always wanted to do this. You're gonna like this girl."

I'm too limp to look around, but the answer comes soon as tall guy begins to rub Angel's cum and mine on my asshole. *Oh, fuck, I've never,* and then as his cock enters my poor abused cunt his fingers work their way into my virgin asshole and suddenly I get the attraction. A million nerve endings, all connected to my spine it feels, wake up and begin to sing. As he works to get my tight hole lubed up, I try to relax the muscles and open up for him.

And then his cock replaces his fingers and oh, my god, it's dirty and kinky and primal and hot. No wonder, no fucking wonder, and there's pain but somehow that makes it better and suddenly tall guy is more than just tall guy, he's my newfound Good-Time Johnny and I begin to howl like a fucking animal, and the orgasm I just rode in on comes back for another trip. Angel has to grab me around the waist, holding me down to the tailgate, to keep me from bucking myself completely off of tall guy's cock. My asshole clamps down with the full force of my orgasm, and now it's tall guy who is howling like a wild animal and suddenly, finally he comes as well and I feel it pouring into my ass as the final spasms wrack through my body.

I lie half sprawled across the tailgate for an eternity it seems. My legs won't hold me up. My ass is on fire and my pussy is numb. My come and theirs intermingle and run down my thighs, and I feel Angel's come drying down the side of my face. My panties are ground into the dirt. Angel has zipped up his pants and gotten back into their truck, and tall guy asks if I need help getting back to my truck.

"I'm Ray, by the way."

Ray, Ray of the Horse Cock. He holds my elbow as I try to stand upright. I'm shaking, a mix of exhaustion and elation.

I stumble back to my truck unassisted. I can't believe cops haven't shown up. What would that arrest be for? Public fuckery? Sodomy? Hell, I don't know. Ray watches me until I start the truck, then gets into his own. They pull away, and I wonder if there are any words spoken between them as they drive home.

My pussy is destroyed and my throat is bruised. As I glance in the rearview, I see the smudged mascara makes me look like I've got twin black eyes. My ass is fucking violated, and one nipple feels like it got caught in a vise.

And I'd do it all over again.

BLUSH

Mary Borsellino

The long black waves of her hair fall over one eye as she ducks her head, looking nervous and almost ashamed. The effect is like a classic movie siren standing before me, with her full, red lips and soft, smooth white skin.

"My dick doesn't really get hard all the way," she explains, apologetic. Her voice is smoky, a little rough, the legacy of too many cigarettes. "Hormones, you know."

We're in her room, a third-floor walkup with the neon and noise of the city on a Friday night just outside the window. She has a poster for the movie *Cabaret* on her wall. She told me at the club that her name is Sally; I have no idea if this is true.

It was a tiny, dirty club, four hours ago. Sally's a singer in a band, the kind of band that wasn't very good but will be one day. Very, very good. She's got the charisma of a future star.

I step forward and kiss her again, to wipe the apology and trepidation from her beautiful face. Her mouth tastes like vodka and Red Bull.

"Lena," she murmurs against my mouth, my vanilla gloss and her berry-tinted makeup a smeared recipe on our lips, "if you aren't okay with this…"

I imagine other lovers from the past, flirtations begun that never got this far: men and women unprepared for this beautiful girl who's more than she appears, homophobes and separatists whose hatred of anything that transgresses their comfort zone is so well known that it gets murder convictions overturned.

No wonder she's hesitant. No wonder she trembles.

I'm the small-boned, feisty sort, the dark little pixie who emerges bruised and elated from every dancing pit. Torn clothes and a brilliant smile. That's how I looked when I approached her at the edge of the stage as she coiled the cord from her microphone around her hand, packing up to go home. I grinned at her; she grinned back.

As far as I was concerned, that was that. Stars, trumpets, the fall at first sight.

I was one smitten kitten from that moment on, but it's clear that Sally needs a little more convincing before she trusts me with the lush and fragile chambers of her heart.

I kiss her again and again and again, a trail of soft presses of my lips over the curve of her jaw, the excited pulse-flutter of her throat. She hums in appreciation when I cup one of her small, perfect breasts through her dress with my hand. The pleased, lazy sound turns to a hiss when I pinch the nipple between my thumb and forefinger.

I maneuver her backward until her shins hit the edge of her mattress, then push her down until she's sitting. Her black-lashed, hazel eyes are dark, her mouth bitten and swollen, her pale cheeks hectic with a flush. She raises her arms obediently so I can lift her dress up over her head, leaving her in the simple bra and panties set she has on underneath.

"I had no idea you could get even more beautiful," I tell her, and sink to my knees.

I've got stuff in one of the spacious pockets of my pants, because I'm a cocky little fucker (no pun intended; I've got a vagina and love it dearly) and I set out with an intention to score tonight. I had no idea I'd end up with a catch as impressive as Sally, but it's always nice to exceed one's own expectations.

There are condoms, and dental dams, both in a variety of synthetic fruit flavors that are only marginally less ridiculous than a mouthful of the basic latex taste. Why they can't make safer sex taste like sex is a constant mystery to me. I love every part of being with another person, the scents of her skin and her sweat, the bitter organic shock of precome or the lush slick palate of a flushed and wanting vulva. If I wanted a mouthful of banana flavor, I'd deep-throat a goddamn banana.

Along with the condoms and the dams, I've got latex gloves and water-based lube. I dump all of it on the soft carpet beside me, and turn my attention to the task of taking Sally's underwear off with my teeth.

The swell of her arousal against the peach-colored cotton makes my mouth water, but I ignore it for the time being and grasp the elastic lace of the waistband between my lips and ease it down, careful and slow.

Like she said it would be, her dick's hard but not iron-firm, the skin still soft and pliable to the touch when I give in to some of my baser instincts and reach one hand up to stroke lightly along the length as I continue my underwear-removing plan with my mouth. It makes her erection seem more vulnerable than others I've seen. It feels as soft as fine velvet against my palm.

"Oh, fuck," Sally chokes, gripping the edge of the mattress with both hands and clearly making a very strong effort not to buck up into the touch. Good thing, too, as her knee would end up in my windpipe if she moved like that right now. I rock back onto my heels and peel her panties down the rest of the way with my hands.

"Do you want me to put on the gloves? I can stimulate your prostate at the same time, if you have trouble with penile orgasms," I offer. Sally's look is adorably bewildered, like she doesn't understand why I'd be making clinical conversation when we could be fornicating instead.

"Uh," she manages, snow-white face furrowed in thought for a moment. "No, that's okay. Next time, maybe. I can mostly come okay without, but there's sometimes not much to show for it when I do."

I nod, smiling happily at her as I tear open the packet on a relatively inoffensive strawberry-flavored condom. "You want a next time?"

She blushes, pressing her lips together. I'm kneeling between her spread legs, her panties around one of her ankles, and I'm about to suck her dick, and she's blushing at being caught out as wanting a second date. She's so perfect I think I'm probably going to end up falling in love with her.

"Yes?" Sally answers. My grin widens, and I kneel up closer to roll down the condom.

"Me, too," I tell her, and then I go down until I'm deep-throating her. The fact that she isn't hard all the way helps, a little, but I don't take that as any excuse to do a halfhearted job at it. I wrap my mouth as hot and tight around her as I can, flexing my throat in small fluttering swallows around the head.

Her pubic hair is coarse and crinkly against my nose and I can stare up just enough to watch the excited, overwhelmed rise and fall of her soft belly as she breathes as best she can. I can't really reach up from this angle to touch her breasts very effectively, but Sally seems to have thought of that already and is rubbing them in slow, dreamlike motions as she watches my mouth work the length of her dick.

I press my tongue up against the thick vein on the underside, liking the way that the latex and the skin between me and Sally's pulse shift together at the movement. I inhale deeply through my nose, chasing the smells of her body and the smells of how turned on she is by my mouth on her, how I'm pushing her closer and closer to the edge of climax with nothing but this simple act. There's no rush of power quite like it in the world, that knowledge that you can make another person come, can release her desire and expose her most secret and vulnerable parts. That's my favorite part of sex.

My jaw's begun to ache, in that good bone-deep way that I know I'll feel tomorrow morning while I brush my teeth and yawn on the subway on my ride in to work. I'll move my mouth just that certain way and feel that soreness, and my body will be flooded with the sense memory of being here, kneeling before her, at this moment.

I'm so turned on that I think I might come without even being touched. My own underwear is damp between my legs and my clit is throbbing, so much so that I have to slip one of my hands down and rub hard against the seam of my pants or I'm going to end up losing my mind from being so horny. My nipples are hard against the inside of my shirt and every suck, every lick I make against Sally's cock, just heightens my own arousal. I'm drooling down my chin, spit-slick against the latex, and can't stop moaning. Her thighs are shaking and her head's thrown back, ruby-red mouth open as she screams my name and comes with one of her hands still digging into the mattress, the other resting on the back of my head.

As the climax shudders through her she pulls my hair, and

the sharp shock of pain in my scalp is enough to trip me over into my own jolt of orgasm. Stars flash black and white behind my eyelids and vertigo sends me reeling for endless seconds of blind pleasure.

When I come back to myself, I'm resting my cheek against Sally's thigh and panting raggedly. I slip the condom off her and tie it, tossing it aside for the time being so that I can crawl up her body, pushing her back until her shoulder blades hit the mattress and we're lying face-to-face.

"That was nice," I tell her, my throat sounding completely fucked-out and wrecked. The sound of it makes her blush again, which makes me laugh and lean in to kiss her. I think I could really fall in love with a girl like this.

THE SPANKING SALON

Elizabeth Coldwell

Everyone on campus knew about the Salon. It was a story that did the rounds in freshers' week, like the one about the history student who had some kind of breakdown during his final exams, and turned in a paper consisting of the word *Aardvark,* repeated over and over on twelve sides of foolscap. But the Salon wasn't an urban legend, it was real—a secret, men-only club where you could watch and participate in the punishment of willing young women. Hence its more commonly used name, the Spanking Salon.

Becoming a member appealed to me on a level I couldn't explain. The thought of a woman having her bottom bared for an intense hand warming, or an extended paddling, turned me on like nothing else. But my chances of stepping through the Salon's door—hell, of even being told the location of those doors—were zero. No one knew quite how the club recruited its prospective members. Some said you had to be spotted browsing the collection of Victorian erotica buried deep in the library stacks. Others that it was a matter of family connections: only if your father had been a member of the Salon would you be admitted. Whatever the criteria for selection were, I knew I'd fail to meet them. That was confirmed the morning invitations to their initiation ceremony were stuffed into the pigeonholes of the lucky few.

Freddie Burleigh, who had the room next to mine and was the closest friend I'd made in my first few weeks at university, was checking his post at the same time as me. The bundle he pulled out included a thick, cream-covered envelope bearing nothing more than his name in neat copperplate handwriting.

"What've you got there?" I asked, watching him browse its contents with growing comprehension.

"You're not going to believe it, Ash. I've been invited to join the Spanking Salon." He thrust his invitation under my nose. Quickly, I scanned the handwritten note, envy gnawing at my gut. The pleasure of his attendance was requested on Friday night, at an address in town I didn't recognize.

"Well done, mate." I fought to keep the jealousy I felt out of my voice. It was no surprise Freddie had been recruited. He was prime Salon material: public school educated; father something in the diplomatic service; handsome in a sturdy, well-bred kind of way. More importantly, I'd seen the paperbacks he kept hidden behind his History of Art course books: lurid pulp novels with pictures of naked, blushing asscheeks on their covers, penned by authors with names like Ophelia Birch and Rosie Bottoms.

Glancing at the mail rack, I saw only one other similar envelope waiting to be collected. Hardly any of the pigeonholes had been emptied, it being Saturday and the lure of a lie-in after last night's excesses appealing more than the indifferent breakfast served up in the refectory. If the number of invitations issued was similar across the university's other five halls of residence, only a dozen or so initiates would be attending the Salon's next meeting. I longed to know who they were, what made them special. And what perverse delights awaited them on Friday night.

Of course, I had no expectation of ever finding out. Freddie might regale me with a watered-down version of events if I pressed him, but I was sure he'd be sworn to keep the real meat a secret. I'd simply have to stew in my frustration, lying on my bed, wanking and thinking of what I was missing.

Until a flu bug swept the hall. Half the people on our floor succumbed, including big, healthy Freddie. When he didn't make it down to breakfast on Friday morning, I popped my head round his door to find him pale-faced and shivering, too weak to make it any farther than the bathroom at the end of the corridor. One look at him and I knew he wouldn't be keeping his appointment at the Salon tonight.

"Anything I can get you on the way back from lectures?" I asked him, my concern genuine. We might have been chalk and cheese, but I really liked the guy.

"Paracetamol and orange juice should do the trick," he croaked in reply. "Thanks, Ashley, you're a true pal."

Instead of the paracetamol, I bought him an over-the-counter flu remedy, designed to soothe his aches, lower his fever and help him sleep. When I checked in on him again at seven, he was dosed up and dead to the world.

I know I shouldn't have taken advantage of him, but I simply couldn't help myself. That morning, I'd seen the tuxedo hanging on his wardrobe door, the outfit he'd planned to wear to the Salon. Along with it was a black domino mask. That gave me the idea. Freddie and I were roughly the same height, even if he was broader in build than me, and we both had short, fair hair. With the mask, in a darkened room, alongside a group of people who didn't know Freddie too well—and, in any case, would be more concerned about their own satisfaction—I reckoned I just might be able to pass for him.

Even so, my hand was shaking as I handed over the invitation, sure my deception would be picked up. The address on the card led me to a building just off one of the town's main shopping streets, with the kind of plain, black-painted door you could walk past a hundred times without ever noticing. I slipped my mask into position, knocked and waited.

The door was opened moments later by a tall, dark-haired man in evening dress, who looked me up and down.

"Yes?" he asked.

"The meeting tonight." I did my best approximation of Freddie's Sloaney drawl. "I have an invitation."

He studied it, then looked back to me. Could he tell I'd altered the fit of Freddie's jacket with strategically placed safety pins, worn an extra pair of socks so his shiny black shoes weren't too big for me and gelled my hair so it fell over as much of my face as possible in an attempt to conceal my real identity?

"Please come in."

Almost punching the air with delight, I followed him inside, through to a room with black walls and bare wooden floorboards, lit only by the light of flickering candles in wrought-iron holders. Masked men in formal wear stood round in twos and threes, chatting and sipping champagne. It struck me this place resembled nothing so much as a miniature version of the gentleman's clubs where discreet networking took place and business deals were struck. A haven where no women intruded and who you knew was more important than what you knew.

Looking at my fellow initiates, I realized any one of them could be someone I saw every day: a student on my course; someone who worked out in the union gym alongside me; one of the volunteers who served behind the Junior Common Room bar. Disguised as they were, I had no way of knowing. But, I reasoned, if I couldn't recognize them, by the same token they couldn't recognize me.

The man who'd let me inside took me over to what I assumed must be the president of this society, judging by the ornate gold mask he wore.

"Freddie Burleigh, Sir."

My hand was grasped in a bone-crushing shake. Slate-gray eyes regarded me from behind the mask. "Freddie, welcome to the Salon. I'm Martyn Salisbury."

The name didn't mean anything to me. I wondered whether Freddie knew him, and settled for a neutral, "It's good to be here," by way of reply.

"You're the last to arrive," he told me. "We were beginning to give up on you, to tell you the truth. You wouldn't have been the first potential initiate to get cold feet at the last minute. But now that you're here the real fun of the evening can begin." Martyn tapped his glass, attracting everyone's attention. Heads swiveled to look at him. "Gentlemen, tonight is a very special night for all of us. Every year, we select the cream of the new university intake to join the ranks of our little society. Tonight, those of you who have only ever dreamed of witnessing a bare-bottomed spanking in the flesh will discover what it really feels like to watch as a girl's ass turns crimson under the loving attentions of a firm hand—and experience the thrill of punishing her yourself."

An excited murmur ran round the room. Everything we'd heard about the Salon was true. This was a haven for spankos, carrying on its business under the noses of our lecturers and professors. Unless, of course, some of them were here tonight, hidden behind masks...

"Would the novitiates step forward to join me, please?"

Already at Martyn's side, I waited as another eight men

made themselves known, almost ashamed of their eagerness in stepping forward. Fewer in number even than I'd expected, we didn't dare to make eye contact for fear of revealing just how stricken with nervous anticipation we were.

"Gentlemen, let me explain the rules for tonight. Allow me to introduce you to the lovely Scarlett."

At his words, a girl of around twenty was led into the room, dressed in a short, flirty white dress decorated with a cute cherry pattern. Her nut-brown hair was fastened in two pigtails at the nape of her neck, and she wore bright red T-bar shoes and white ankle socks. She looked the very picture of innocence, but a glint in her eye told me a saucy little pain slut lurked beneath the carefully constructed façade. Was she a student, taking part in tonight's ceremony for the love of it, or a working girl with a taste for submission? It didn't really matter. She clearly wanted to be spanked every bit as much as Martyn Salisbury and his cronies wanted to spank her.

A high-backed chair was set down in the center of the room, the other members of the Salon forming a partial circle around it. At Martyn's command, we took our places, completing the circle.

"First, you will watch as Scarlett is treated to a thorough bottom warming. Then each of you will have the opportunity to give her six of the best. Think of it, gentlemen, six hard spanks on her peachy, perfect cheeks…"

Glancing at the guys on either side of me as Martyn talked us through the pleasures to come, I couldn't help noticing they both already had distinct swellings in their evening trousers. I couldn't blame them; who could fail to be aroused in such surroundings, with the prospect of dishing out their first-ever spanking growing closer?

His speech at an end, Martyn sat on the chair, ordering Scarlett to drape herself over his knee. She made a halfhearted attempt to resist him, but it was all part of the game. Martyn simply grasped her wrist and hauled her into place. He'd made sure to position himself so the initiates had the perfect view of her round, plump ass, the dress straining across its curves. Edging up the hem, ignoring her protests that he simply couldn't do such a thing to her, he revealed Scarlett's white cotton panties, the spanking fetishist's undergarment of choice. Their crotch looked damp; proof, if any more was really needed, that she was enjoying this ritual every bit as much as we were.

"So, do you have anything to say for yourself before your spanking begins?" Martyn asked.

Scarlett's reply was simple and heartfelt. "Please, Sir, I need to be punished."

"Then punished you shall be. By me and my nine associates. I hope you're ready for that." Everyone in the room seemed to hold his breath as Martyn drew back his arm. A moment's tense silence, then his hand landed with an audible crack on Scarlett's panty-clad ass.

She gave a little "Ow," even though the blow didn't seem that hard. Still, it was what we expected. What we wanted.

Martyn repeated the action on Scarlett's other cheek, bringing another little mew of pain from her. Somewhere to my left, I heard a groan—part desire, part disappointment—and wondered whether the excitement had caused one of my fellow first-timers to come before the real fun started.

Ignoring the noise, Martyn concentrated on giving Scarlett's ass what my mother would have called a good skelping, slapping her cheeks hard through the thin underwear, over and over again. We didn't need to be told we were watching a maestro in action. His spanking motion was smooth, the strokes unhurried, giving the anticipation just enough time to build before the next one fell. For Scarlett's part, she wriggled prettily on his knee in reaction to her punishment, the crotch of her panties, aided by Martyn's thick fingers, slipping into the groove between her pussy lips to give us a glimpse of the delights to come once he pulled them down fully.

I heard the rasp of a zipper coming down, and glanced over to see the guy to my right extracting his cock from his fly. My companion to my left already had his dick out—as, it appeared, did everyone watching except me.

Martyn had noticed it, too. All the time, I thought he'd been concentrating on Scarlett and her reactions to the spanking, but it appeared he'd had an eye on his audience, too.

"A little slow in joining us there, Freddie." His tone made it obvious he expected me to be wanking publicly by now. "Don't tell me you're shy? And you a good Cavendish School boy, too. They're usually the first to start the circle jerks."

He was waiting, as was everyone in the room, but I couldn't bring myself to unzip my trousers. Not here, not in front of all these people I didn't know.

When my hand didn't move in the direction of my fly, Martyn decided matters should be taken into someone else's hands. He spoke to the initiate on my right. "Why don't you help Freddie out, Smith? He's obviously having first night nerves. Though I don't know why. After all, it's not as though he's going to have anything we haven't all seen before…"

This was the last thing I'd expected to happen, to have fingers other than my own undressing me. I tried to stop Smith grabbing for my zipper, but I was too slow. He pushed a hand inside my borrowed evening trousers, seeking for a hard, aching cock—and finding only wet, puffy pussy-flesh.

His baffled surprise lasted only a moment. "Fuck me!" he bellowed, alerting everyone else to his discovery. "Freddie's a girl!"

Trying to back out of the circle, I was grabbed by Smith, who looked like he played rugby and had the brute strength to prove it. Without ceremony, Martyn dumped Scarlett off his lap and strode over to me.

"What's going on here?" He tugged the domino mask from my face, staring into my wide, panicked eyes. "Who are you, and where's Freddie?"

"I...my name's Ashley Powell," I admitted. "I'm a friend of Freddie's. He's ill, so I borrowed his invitation. I'm sorry I deceived you, but there was no other way I was going to be allowed into the Salon, and I wanted to come here so badly. I know I shouldn't have."

"Damn right you shouldn't. This place has secrets, secrets generations of Salon members have worked very hard to keep hidden over the years, and in you barge in your stolen clothes, spying on things that were never meant for the eyes of someone like you." For the first time, I became aware of Martyn's height, at six foot four a good six inches taller than me, and the way his muscular body bulked out his tuxedo. So strong, so dominant. His dark eyes stared into mine, and in that moment he knew me. "Of course, you know there's only one thing to do with someone who lies and cheats her way in here, don't you?"

I dropped my gaze, aware of a mounting excitement in the room. "Y-yes, Sir."

Martyn turned to Scarlett, who'd almost been forgotten about in all the ruckus following the revelation of my real identity. "I'm afraid we won't be needing you any longer, sweetheart. Someone will call you a taxi. Don't worry, there'll be a little something extra in your tribute by way of compensation."

So she was a tart—and a very disappointed one, from her petulant pout as she was escorted from the room. Still, it left the way clear for Martyn to focus on dealing with me. I shifted from foot to foot, nervously awaiting his next instructions. They weren't long in coming, but to my surprise, they weren't directed at me.

"Gentlemen, as you all now know, we have an intruder. A very cunning one, but one who needs to be punished for this show of audacity. And the first thing we have to show her is that taking someone's clothes without permission is wrong. Smith, Berry, remove that stolen outfit from her, would you?"

"But I didn't steal it, I just—" I tried to protest, as Smith and the ginger-haired lad who'd been standing to my left began to unbutton my jacket. Just like Scarlett's, my protests were part of the game. Try as I might to deny it, my pussy was pulsing, fluid with desire as the two initiates stripped me of Freddie's clothing.

Shoes, socks, jacket, trousers, bow tie, shirt—all were removed from me in a matter of moments. I'd used bandages to flatten my breasts and aid in the illusion I was male, though in truth there wasn't too much to conceal. With a contemptuous flick of his wrist, Smith disposed of the fastenings keeping them in place. They slithered to the floor, baring my tits to the assembled guests. It was the most humiliating moment of my life, yet I'd never been so turned on. Martyn couldn't have known my most potent fantasies involved being stripped before a punishment while an audience looked on, though I'd never dreamed I'd ever find myself in this position.

Berry caught hold of my panties, preparing to lower them.

"Hey!" I objected. "Those are mine, not Freddie's."

Martyn chuckled. "That may be so, but naughty girls who lie and steal shouldn't be allowed to keep them on. Otherwise they'll never learn their lesson, will they?"

With that, he told Berry to pull my underwear down. I stood meekly as the shamefully damp garment was passed from man to man, eager noses sniffing at the cotton.

I attempted to cover my bare crotch with my hands, but Martyn ordered me to link my fingers behind my head so everyone in the room could take a good look at my naked state. "You're enjoying this entirely too much," he said, even though my cheeks burned with shame. "Maybe that will change once you're over my knee."

Taking me by the hand, he led me over to the chair. Sitting down, he guided me efficiently into position, rump upraised. Unlike Scarlett, I didn't try to resist. What was the point in pretending I didn't want this, that all the time I'd been preparing to watch another woman being punished, I'd been thinking how it would feel if I was the one whose ass was on the receiving end? I differed from everyone else who'd stepped through the door of the Salon for the first time tonight not just because I was female and they were male. They'd always wanted to give a spanking, but I'd always wanted to take one.

"Before we go any further, Ashley, do you have anything to say for yourself?"

"Only that I'm sorry, Sir."

"Believe me, you're not sorry yet, but you will be when this is over. As the stand-in for Scarlett, you'll be expected to take the same punishment she would. I shall be warming you up, then six spanks from each of the initiates."

It was a lot to expect a novice like me to take, but as Martyn's hand caressed the curves of my ass, acquainting itself with the texture and weight of my flesh, I willed him not to push me past my limits.

The circle of masked men had reconvened around us, clutching their cocks as they waited for my punishment to begin. For a moment, I gazed at them, proud and defiant. I'd infiltrated their all-male environment, breaking their rules, and I was unrepentant about that fact. Indeed, I'd have no qualms about doing it again.

My defiance lasted as long as it took Martyn to land the first smack. His open palm made contact with my bare ass, stinging more than I'd believed possible. When I yelled, it wasn't a cursory acknowledgment of the slap, like Scarlett's had been. It had bloody hurt, and I wanted everyone to know it.

Martyn's tone held a certain smug satisfaction. "Wasn't what you thought it would be, was it? Are you starting to regret this now?" His words were punctuated with smacks, each equally hard as the first. Falling in the same spot every time, they burned, making me writhe against the harsh twill of his trousers—and the substantial bulge lurking at his crotch. With every blow, the fists of our audience moved faster on their cocks, the sights and sounds of my punishment spurring them on to make themselves come.

But even though my spanking was so much more painful than I'd ever dreamed, already the endorphins were doing their best to soothe the hurt, and I was riding a wave of sweet, dark bliss. "No, Sir, I don't regret it," I told him.

"Well, I've done my best," he replied, even though I was sure the spanking he'd given me was only a fraction of what he could dish out, should he choose. "Let's see what someone else can do. Smith, would you like to take your turn?"

And so began my long, drawn-out punishment at the hands of the initiates. One by one, they stepped up to take Martyn Salisbury's place. A couple approached me with a measure of assurance, even if they didn't really feel it, while the others were endearingly clumsy in their eagerness to spank me. Each ordered me onto his lap, searching for the same authoritative tone Martyn had used. They stroked my ass, feeling the heat radiating from it. Some went further, letting a finger slip between my pussy lips to find the wetness there, rubbing my clit or exploring my juicy hole. One of them even slicked his thumb with my cream, before pushing it up my asshole. At least one of the wanking onlookers shot his spunk at the moment I cried out at the shamefully delicious feeling of being penetrated there.

Whatever else they did to me, they all made sure to treat me to six spanks. Most were tentative at first, but by the sixth, they were swinging their arms with confidence, palms falling with unerring accuracy on my sore, blotchy cheeks.

By the end, tears were rolling down my face, and my ass felt so hot and swollen I knew I'd have to sleep on my front that night. Between them, these men had broken me down, but in their appreciation of my submission, the resilience with which I'd taken all they had to give me, they'd put me back together stronger and more alive than before.

What happened now? I wondered, as the last of the initiates helped me off his lap. Did I get down on my knees and suck every single one of them until they came, by way of thanks?

It seemed not. "Thank you, gentlemen," Martyn said, applauding their work. The other members of the Salon joined in, welcoming their new brothers in spanking. "And that concludes the evening's proceedings. I look forward to seeing you again in a month's time." As they began to zip themselves up and prepare to leave, presumably to spend the rest of the night reliving what they'd just witnessed, he turned to me. "As for you, Miss Powell, we still have unfinished business…"

He waited until everyone else had left, letting me wonder what else he had in mind for me. Unzipping his fly, he brought out the only cock I hadn't yet seen. His self-restraint was amazing, not to have touched himself at any point, despite the punishment scene he'd orchestrated so spectacularly. I'd gained some idea of his dimensions as I squirmed on his lap, but still I smiled at my first sight of that long, unyielding column of flesh.

"Suck it," he ordered.

Without a murmur, I sank down, taking him deep in my

mouth. All my gratitude at having been chastised so thoroughly and so publicly was expressed by my lips and tongue, sucking and slurping from root to tip. He tasted of spice and brine, and when I gazed up I saw his eyes half closed, his expression one of wonder. Grazing my teeth along his length, I gave him a teasing hint of how it felt to have your pleasure mingled with sweet pain.

Unable to deny myself what I'd been craving since Martyn's hand first caressed my bare ass, I dabbed at my clit. He realized what I was doing and laughed.

"Greedy girl, aren't you?" Those were the last coherent words he managed before his orgasm overtook him. Fingers curled in my hair, he held my head steady as his load jetted down my throat, his willpower no match for my oral skills. The taste, the feel of him climaxing in my mouth was all it took to have me coming, too, the perfect end to this most extraordinary evening.

As I was dressing to leave, Martyn surprised me with his next words. "So we'll see you in a month, Ashley."

"I'm sorry?" The last thing I'd expected was to be allowed anywhere near the Salon's premises again.

"It's always nice to find a girl who loves to be spanked as much as you do, and who doesn't expect to be paid for the privilege. And after tonight's performance, I think a few of our older members are going to want the opportunity to warm that gorgeous ass of yours. Oh, and bring Freddie with you. He's still got to pass the initiation, after all."

Poor Freddie. I had some explaining to do, when he was well enough to hear it. He'd be annoyed when he realized how I'd used him to get what I wanted. Annoyed enough to punish me? Despite the dull throb of my recently punished ass, I couldn't help hoping so. And with any luck, I wouldn't have to wait 'til the next Salon gathering rolled 'round to learn how that felt.

ON THE VERGE

Rosalia Zizzo

A Doritos bag whirls like a tornado through the parking lot, sprinkling crumbs around cars and empty parking spaces. A quartet of seagulls attacks the bag for what they hope will be a feast, and they squawk and snatch the bag from one another, shaking what is left to the ground. One gull shoves his beak inside, envelops his whole head, then hops like a two-legged Doritos bag toward a snickering Josie at the stadium entrance, who mutters to herself, "Best if you share, guys. Believe me." The corners of her mouth curl, and she shakes her head.

Wiping her forehead with the back of her hand and cradling her binder on her hip, Josie blows her hair out of her eyes and steps into the dark tunnel that leads to her favorite pastime. Wearing her white peasant blouse off the shoulders hasn't made her any cooler. It only draws attention to Josie's obvious sensuality and her need for male attention. Remembering the success of the last ball game, she giggles to herself and prepares for what's to come.

The seagulls continue their feud in the parking lot as she walks with purpose—swaying her blue-jeaned hips—into the stadium that bursts with sunlight when she emerges from the tunnel. Casting her eyes over her surroundings, Josie notices a smattering of people clothed in blue and gold yakking with their friends and munching on stadium snacks, and just as she spots one of her men, she grins while biting her lower lip. The San Diego Padres don't draw a full house, but Josie and her friends watch anyway, their addiction making it impossible to keep away. On the benches sit local fans, drunken businessmen, escapees from the weekly drudgery—those who spend their days in offices and windowless rooms—and students like Josie and the boys.

Josie sees David's blue cap and quickly slides in so they sit hip to hip as he turns his head to observe her clutch her three-ring binder filled with notes and run her tongue over her lips.

"Hey."

"Hey, yourself." David smiles and nudges her arm. "How're you?"

"I'm so hot," she rasps, fanning herself with the binder.

"Yes," he groans, bending his mouth to her ear. "You are." He lifts his head and looks at Josie with heat in his eyes while she continues to fan herself. "Why do you always bring your schoolwork to the game? Why do you even bother?" He gives her a look.

Josie tosses her head back, shrugs, and laughs. "Just something to do in case I get bored. Wink wink." Her eyes meet his, and she jabs his bearish arm as she raises her head to see Doug step over the bench and sandwich her in the middle. Two thick shoulders and firm thighs imprison her in the seat. David adjusts his cap and nods to Doug.

"Hey, Doug."

"Hey, David. Josie." More fanning. "How are you two?"

"Good."

"I'm just so hot."

"Oh, yeah," Doug agrees. "You definitely are." He joins David in bobbing his head.

"You two are so incorrigible," Josie sighs.

"That's right," Doug agrees. "We are very enCOURAGE-able." The guys laugh, and Josie rolls her eyes.

"Ready?"

"Yup."

"Think so."

The boys share more than alliterative names. Both sturdy football players with tree trunks for legs and an anaconda's hug are a vision of the all-American male: thick, meaty shoulders; angular jaws; both in snug jeans and red-and-black San Diego State sweatshirts. The face of Montezuma stares from both chests. Their arms could carry a dozen Josies. They shovel mouthfuls of food through their lips and not an ounce of fat protrudes from their steam-engine torsos. Pure muscle. The answer to Josie's every desire. They tackle each other like tanks, and they handle Josie with care but also with the strength she craves. Nothing but their hard, hot flesh can satisfy her needs, not even a bouquet of brightly colored dildos purchased at the local smut shop.

"Please," she mutters when she feels the tingling begin between her thighs. "Please give it to me. I need it. I deserve it." A warm glow travels to her gut where she feels a heavy weight settling firmly and butterflies fluttering furiously. Moisture collects and pools at the entrance to her cunt. With a one-track mind, Josie ponders human anatomy and what kinky things to do with that anatomy as she sees the balls and bats. She likes to feel the balls of her men slapping her pussy lips repeatedly like last week in the library, bending over the table. But today she wants something a little different. She wants to feel the hard equipment push into her backside while she bends over, pushing backward, and she wants the guys to enter her in a tight, juicy hole a little higher than they're used to. She wants to bend as if in prayer, as if she were offering her body, and for the guys to give her absolution because sex is her religion.

The threesome watch Padres with tight pants running, throwing balls and patting each other's butts. Of course, a real padre would be like a priest, and traditionally, a priest is the minister of divine worship, emptying his life of everything but his spirit and connection to a higher power. He teaches us we are nothing but our divine relationship. Our identity gets wiped clean. We are not our job, our G.P.A., our age, our name, our genetic makeup or our addictions. And yet, addiction is what brings Josie and her two men together.

"What's that joke about priests?" David smirks wickedly and slugs Doug in the shoulder. Doug shrugs and shakes his head. "You know. They thought it was 'celebrate,' but it was really 'celibate.' Talk about feeling ripped off, man!" He pounds Doug again.

"Ha ha ha ha... Yeah." Doug nods in agreement. "I think I actually did hear that one before."

Josie eyes David's swollen bicep and feels her heart jump and a twinge of anticipation.

"Good one, huh?"

"Yeah. Have you heard this one? 'I thought about becoming a monk when I was younger, but I decided not to because I was CLOISTERphobic.'"

"Oh. Another good one. You just want to PUNish us." Doug grins, chuckles, and flags a snack vendor. "Want anything, you guys? I know it's junk, but I'm starving."

"No thanks." David shakes his head.

"I'm always hungry," says Josie. "But I don't think my stomach's empty. It's something else." Both men turn to her with raised eyebrows, rapt. Unthinking, she spreads her legs slightly. At times, she behaves like an empty-headed bimbo: slutty, ready to jump into bed with anyone. She acts like the stereotypical blonde, yet her tresses could not be confused with anything but brunette. Josie is short for Josefina. Sepia-toned photos of her sour-faced family arriving on Ellis Island prove her true colors.

The ballpark is a simple location. It always has been. The three friends hint to one another of what's to immediately follow: Doug winks, David jokes and smiles, and Josie licks her lips. They meet regularly, weekly even, to fulfill their basest desires in whatever fashion will successfully satisfy their gnawing cravings. Josie grabs one of David's fries and pops it in her mouth while leering at Doug and chewing slowly, making a show of licking the catsup from each finger.

Mewling softly, Josie reaches her hand past Doug's face, grazes his cheek and fiddles with his hair. At the same time, she places her other hand in David's lap, running her index finger along the length of him through the denim, and as his erection hardens further, she feels a knot growing in her gut. Her appetite increases as she unzips David's tight jeans, fondles his warmth and feels him grow firmer. Tempted to climb into his lap with her escalating hunger, she takes a deep breath and looks at Doug.

Doug wolfs down his hot dog, gulps his beer and avoids the terrorizing seagulls. He leans into Josie's now-aggressive petting with his head and sucks her earlobe when he's done swallowing.

"Ooo. God, your tongue is awesome." She looks like a cat enjoying a scratch behind the ears. She loves to watch him chew and swallow. That gulp, that thick, moving throat tempts her and makes her body tug from the inside.

"Hey, Josie," Doug says hoarsely with a smirk. "Look." He glances down at his own lap where his bulge mimics David's.

"Oh, boy," Josie says, and chuckles. Her binder falls to the sticky ground as she works both hands around both cocks.

"We'll have to be fast once we get there so…" After Josie grants him access to her pussy by spreading her legs farther, David unbuttons and unzips her jeans. She gazes into his dark eyes while he slides his finger along the slit and moves slow circles around her already slick clit, gradually increasing his pace so that it matches that of her stroking. Josie moans and licks her lower lip. "That's it, gorgeous," he tells her as he draws his finger toward the front along with a generous pool of thick cream. "You are so ready." She looks into his eyes. David's mother being Japanese adds an exotic look to his face that Josie finds thrilling.

Twenty-five hundred years ago the Buddha is said to have attained Sunyata: he freed himself from anything worldly clinging to him and achieved significance in the great void. Looking at the baseball diamond is like looking into a void, the void. If you are a nihilist, baseball would not release you from worldly suffering, nor would a hot dog from a wandering vendor or a priest's forgiveness for multiple sins. In Sunyata, you find peace in the absence of all that is worldly. You find relief in nothingness. Josie finds relief in sex. She can empty her life of all meaningless waste when she meets with her men, and she can exist in a world where nothing else matters. The world disappears. No more school, no more worries, no past, no future. Just now.

David grips Josie's wrist, ceasing her fervent stroking, and lets out a strong sigh. "Jesus." His eyes roll up for a moment. "Stop. Let's go." He grunts and tugs Josie's arm as he stands. He does a quick tuck and zip while Josie closes her own jeans and reaches into her pocket to palm a pinkie-length packet of lube. Both men adjust their jeans that have grown so tight in the front there is no question as to what they want. They have to hurry. After rushing up the stairs, they usher Josie into the men's restroom, where, after checking that it's empty, David hangs his black market CLOSED FOR MAINTENANCE placard.

All three rush in. As the game continues with cheers from the crowd, the men squeeze Josie between them inside the doorway and explore her body, running their hands up and down while kissing her mouth. They alternate between massaging her body and pressing their lips to hers, nuzzling any exposed skin around her throat. David breathes into her pulsating neck while Doug places his palm on one of her braless breasts under the blouse with his fingers at her nipple. Josie gnaws the necks and mouths of the two men while enjoying their male flesh and muscular bodies. Twisting her head back and forth, Josie devours the guys before moving them closer to the sink where she can grip the hard surface to steady herself as she bends over.

"You know what I want," she says. "In the ass."

Doug inhales sharply. "Unbelievable." He jerks his head toward David and back again while whispering, "You really are the hottest woman I've ever known."

David nods his agreement while breathing, "Yeah."

Josie tosses David the lube, which he hastily opens with his teeth. Josie leans over the basin, facing the mirror, and grips the edges as David unbuttons, unzips and yanks down her jeans, kicking her legs apart after letting her pull one leg free. She bends her body lower so that the guys can see their target and exhales while she turns her head to look at their approach. Both guys stare at that juicy pink swirl, that glistening red vortex, that hypnotic hot aperture in their line of vision for a moment. While Doug moves to stand watch at the door, David releases himself from his jeans, strokes himself furiously with an ample squirt of lube and hesitantly enters Josie from behind.

Josie feels his wet acorn-tip toy at the rim before punching through. She yelps while raising her face to the sky then growls as he reaches around to finger her swollen clit while slowly pushing into the taut hole.

"So tight," he breathes as he buries himself into her, sliding thick and full completely to her core, filling the void, filling the emptiness, giving her a moment of intense relief and satisfaction after a second of pain. Pushing backward, she feels drops of sweat hitting her back and David leaning against her so his body molds to hers. As he wraps her in his arms while employing his fingers to massage her clit with a puddle of lube mixed with her own warm juices, he whimpers as he restrains himself from pounding into her.

Even so, Josie wants to thrust backward. Pain is far from her mind. All she can think about is his slick finger and that she doesn't want it to stop moving. Already, she can feel the tingling climb up her shoulders. She wants to drive toward the end and feel the fireworks explode throughout her body.

"You're so wet." His breath comes faster. "How is it possible?"

With his middle finger, David strokes her swollen folds and runs delicious circles around her clit while Josie looks into the mirror to see her own flushed face.

"Oh, yeah," she exhales. Her eyes and open mouth exhibit sweet torment. She clenches her teeth. "Please." She bucks against him harder as he circles his finger faster. "I deserve it."

A round of cheering causes Doug to glance furtively out the door and whip his head around whispering, "Hurry it up, guys. We have to be fast."

"More," Josie whimpers. "Please."

Holding his breath, David pumps with more need until he

empties into her and exhales with a long groan into her hair. He thrusts twice more and rocks. When he's completely spent and has quickly cleaned her backside and himself with a paper towel, he trades places with Doug, who uses the remainder of the lube packet before throwing it into the trash.

Josie observes her own restlessness and whimpers into the mirror. "Hurry. Now," she pleads at Doug's eyes and looks at the strands of her hair caught in a few coarse whiskers.

Doug squeezes into her and, even in their haste, they move with determination. He licks his fingers and reaches around Josie's hips to touch her while he slides in and out, stroking that spot just along the length of her clit that has swelled into its own appendage. He rubs her with two fingers just at her entrance, just around the clit, and pushes into her slowly from behind so she can feel him on her back and force her closer to the sink, making Josie plead at her face in the mirror.

"Oh, pleeeease."

Josie glimpses Doug's eyes in the mirror again and senses the impending culmination to their efforts. She's so close. Just there. A few more thrusts and a few more strokes to go.

"Don't stop," she groans through each thrust.

Doug's stamina proves worthwhile, as Josie watches herself contract in climax and sees her own face in the mirror, glossy. "Yesss!" she cries as she clamps down on her jaw, her hands squeeze the sink and her hair sticks to her clammy cheeks and forehead. Small beads of sweat dot her upper lip and temples. She whimpers while Doug finishes her and gives one final push, and she feels him pulse inside her. She holds her breath before letting it go loudly, jerking her shoulders, buckling at the knees. Her palms ache and tingle from the hard, concrete basin. They both continue to groan and sigh as their bodies gradually descend into relaxation.

In the evening, Josie has trouble sleeping. Her schoolbooks stare at her from her desk, and she feels a void only sex can fill. Although still sore, she wants to beg the boys for another fix. Some must have a manicure, diet soda or a newspaper tabloid. For others, it's television or religion. For some, it's food. For Josie it's sex. In the barren, musty stacks of the fifth floor of the library, in Doug's bed, David's Jacuzzi, or in the stadium restroom, relief comes when you know nothing in this world can possibly complete you, and you don't care anyway. Sex is her answer to any question. When you float in abandon before scattering into a million pieces throughout the universe like chips in a parking lot, you know that being on the verge of an earth-shattering, mind-blowing climax is really all there ever truly is.

Reflecting on the day, Josie decides she has delayed long enough. Smiling to herself, she picks up the phone.

SUSANNA

Krissy Kneen

Susanna had a talent with words. This fact came as a surprise to her because for the most part her life had been shrouded in silence. Her first language was Auslan, one of the hand-signal languages invented to communicate with the deaf. Her tiny baby's hands pulled rhythmically on invisible teats when she was hungry, milking the air. Her mother, a silent beauty smelling of milk and lavender, responded to her call by lifting one swollen breast out of her floral dress.

Spoken words were useless in Susanna's home. Her parents' hands could shout out commands, punish her naughtiness or soothe her into sleep with hand-stories of little girls in the forest and big bad wolves made of hooked claw-fingers. Her name was a collection of letters spelled out on her fingertips. It was a difficult word for a little girl to pronounce without the benefit of sound. She could spell it clumsily at first, but her mother pointed to the framed painting hung above her bed, *Susanna and the Elders* by Artemisia Gentileschi.

S-u-s-a-n-n-a, her mother spelled out, her fingers graceful. She pointed to her daughter. *Susanna,* she spelled out again. The painting and the girl. Later, Susanna peered at the painting, the naked young woman illuminated by the spill from the moon. The girl in the painting attempted to hold a bedsheet up to cover her breasts. Two clothed men stared at her and although they seemed more thoughtful than lustful, something about the way they looked at her was unsettling. Susanna held her own bedsheet up, covering one of her own small breasts, imitating her namesake. The other was exposed to the moonlight. She imagined the two men hiding in the shadows and a delicious thrill, half fear, half pleasure, began to warm her stomach. She pulled the blanket up over her nakedness and closed her eyes tight, but whenever she peeked up at the painting, Susanna was always there. Naked; exposed.

She entered the world of spoken words hesitantly, her silence often misinterpreted as shyness. While the other children screamed and shouted, Susanna sat quietly, watching. The world of school was a barrage of noise. She sat through each day longing for the silent relief of home.

For her final assignment at university she made a silent film, a tribute to the older examples of the craft. In Susanna's film the women expressed their passion with a fist held to the breast. The men responded with a widening of the eyes. Her assessors were confused. *No words?* they wrote beside her final grade. *Perhaps you could have at least provided some emotive music.* She left university for the last time stepping out into noisy peak-hour traffic, wondering what exactly she was meant to do.

For a time she helped at a school for hearing-impaired children, breezing from one gloriously quiet classroom to another, distributing cartridge paper and pots of paint. The children were not silent, they clattered and thumped like any children, they grunted and screeched occasionally. But eventually they would settle into a comfortable hush, and Susanna settled with them, completely content.

It was at this school that she met the man who would become her only lover, a deaf man, recently divorced. He had custody of his profoundly deaf son every second week and on the weeks in between Susanna would climb silently into his neatly turned-out bed. They would use their hands to break the silence, making words that were nothing but a dance of the fingers, a barely discernible sliding between the Auslan word for sex and the physical expression of the act itself.

David was a good lover, expressive. His fingers demonstrated to her what he could not say. His mouth, passive throughout the day, was put to better use in the evenings. His lips formed shapes that spoke to her body as words could not. His tongue found ways to express his desire without the use of vowels and consonants. She learned from him a language of love that was as utterly different from the general machinations of sex as Auslan is different from English itself.

The affair, Susanna's first taste of love, stretched out through glorious months into ecstatic years. In this time there was only his body. She knew a little of his working life and shared a proud joy in the academic achievements of his son. But their evenings every second week were reserved almost exclusively for pleasure. It came as some surprise, therefore, when he turned up at her door on an off-week. She glimpsed the sweet purity of his son's profile in the front seat of the parked car.

What I have with her, he signed, his mouth moving to form words he could not speak, *is a real relationship*. Susanna watched his lips and remembered what they had done to her body. The silent words mouthed into her most intimate places, the way her body would answer, silently, but completely. Lifting and opening to him, readying itself for the conversation with the glistening moisture of anticipation.

What I have with you is sex. The most amazing sex, the most wonderful physical expression one body can give to another. But ultimately I suppose I need more than just sex.

Susanna stood in the entryway to the apartment block. It was a wintry evening and she hadn't brought a coat down. She still held her mobile phone with the words lit up on the screen: *I need to speak with you. I am outside your building. Can you come down?*

She remembered the first night with him, the great unveiling. He had spread her legs and knelt at the side of the bed. She should have felt shy, had been expecting to, but somehow his silence and his gentle pressure, parting her thighs, calmed her and filled her with a rush of desire for him. He was watching her closely and suddenly she felt like that other Susanna, Gentileschi's Susanna, revealing more of her body to his gaze than she concealed.

He placed his finger at the edge of her hymen and with his touch she felt the wetness flooding past its shut-tight gate. That single finger felt like his whole body pushing into her. The tip of the lips, the teeth, the tongue and she was slippery as a fish and just as agitated, wriggling her hips to take more of him inside her. Just one finger at first but when it was completely inside she felt stretched to breaking and yet desperate for more.

He seemed amazed by her, amazed by her virginity and her body's impatience to be rid of it. His face so close to the part of her that no one else had ever seen, watching her. He made the sign for *slow down*, both hands held out as if to measure the surface of something reclining, the right hand tilting up as if to halt her progress. *Slow down, slow down,* but even the act of signing was too much of a pause for her. Susanna lifted her hips, taking the stop sign of his hand and pressing it into herself. So much slipperiness. So much sensation, the joy and pain of it fused, too much to bear, her blood slick on his fingers, his body quickly pressing forward into the path that they had newly discovered. He shifted; the gorgeous pressure of his pubic bone pressing where only moments before his tongue had been. Blood on her chest where he took her breast in his fist, blood on her face where she kissed him. She opened herself to him in a pact of spilled blood and when he came there was a second tearing, the condom destroyed, the pact sealed with the jet of his seed finding its way into her, a glorious tragedy, and they remained fused like this, slippery with sweat and blood and ejaculate and every movement of his hips fed her hunger again.

She remembered this as she watched him walk back to his car. Their similar faces turning toward her, the innocence of father and son staring at her for a final time. A twin good-bye. And then they were gone.

Her job as a sound assistant suited her well enough. It was because of the silence. Sometimes her only task in a day would be to drive from place to place collecting silences in her microphone. Ambient sound. She wore soft padded headphones that completely obliterated the world and with a flick of the switch she captured the sounds of empty places. It was not silence, because in this world there is never a total absence of sound. Instead she heard the location speak to her. Houses laid out their quietly settling floorboards, the tick of sunlight on roofs, the low growl of traffic held off by walls and glass and distance. Outdoor places spoke to her with leaf-rustling and grass-twitching, birds swooped in to add their comment to the sense of space, insects chirruped and clicked. Water dripped after rain; gurgled, almost mechanical, through a creek bed.

The empty spaces she recorded provided a leveling effect for films. The steady hum of life formed a meditative background against which the action could take place. Sometimes Susanna had to sit through a performance itself, checking the levels on the little VU dial as the actors ran through their scene time after time. It was a job that could be performed just as easily, she thought, by her ex-lover, a job for the eyes. And because of this she would put her big soft headphones on but not plug them into the equipment. She watched the rise and fall of the needles, adjusted the switches accordingly.

"Did you like that last take?" The actor who approached her was tall and too well muscled. She blinked at him through a fog of silence, reading his lips rather than listening to his words. She nodded, although she had no opinion either way. The needle twitched in the right manner three quarters of the way up the gauge, just as it had twitched on every other take; therefore all of the performances were similarly acceptable. When the actor tried again to make conversation, Susanna felt cornered. What did he want? She had never learned the truth about her beauty, the thick dark hair, the eyes so pale that they were almost unnerving, the body, rounded in the places where it mattered. She had never had the interest to notice the way men tracked her with their gaze as she walked home, head down, full of purpose.

"People always say I could do radio. As a soundo, what do you reckon?" the actor said to her then, and she was forced to slip the headphones off. The sound of the world assaulted her, the actor's rich over-trained voice.

"I need to record the atmos now," she told him, and overhearing her, the first assistant director began to hush the milling crowd, giving Susanna the noise-filled silence that she needed to complete her task.

* * *

Susanna spoke when spoken to, a necessary exchange of meaningless words. Even the deaf are required to do this much to move around in the world. At home she sometimes played soft melancholy music whilst preparing careful dinners for one in her tiny kitchen, but mostly she preferred the quiet.

Her talent for words came to Susanna as a surprise, discovered quite by accident at the same time as she discovered the men. She had been thinking of David. She often thought about him. Since his departure she took her pleasure in a precise, solitary manner. She imagined herself back to her initial unraveling, the moment of pure discovery, her body opening to someone else, the rush as he came, a surprise full of excitement and terror. But on this occasion it occurred to her that she had no photographs of him. It was a simple thing to type his name into her computer; she wondered why she had not thought of it before. A picture of his face would be enough, she expected, to transport her. Of course it would be impossible to find him. His name was a common one and her browser filtered through every option, hooking on a million events and people that might or might not have had some relationship to the David who was the object of her desire. She chose one at random, a school journal, someone too young and too fresh faced. Another, the sale of a motorbike to someone with the same name but not the same temperament as the one she loved.

The third option was the turning point, as they would have said at work. The moment when the dark heart of the story was revealed, the actors turning on their better natures, chasing some false goal and tripping down the path of adventure or folly, racing toward their ultimate demise.

This third click of her finger brought the world to her in vivid color. This other David materialized in her room. It was the same name, but certainly not the same man. This David's body was turning toward fat, and his skin, darker than the love of her life's, came from a warmer climate, some place equatorial. Perhaps it was still there, for it was peppered with a glisten of sweat. A fine dusting of dark hair damp against almost-black nipples. And this man's penis bore no similarity to the only member she had already met. This one was thick and meaty, the slightly flaccid flesh sponging out from short thick fingers, a blanket of skin surrounding it, a fat protective sock that lent the little protrusion inside all the tenderness of a startled animal.

But as she watched, the animal grew bold, thrusting its head out of its hiding place, abandoning its blanket. She stared, transfixed, uncertain if this man with the same name as the gentle lover of her memory was an actor or a phantom of some previous moment, endlessly replayed on the merry-go-round of the World Wide Web. His greeting startled her. He leaned forward with his free hand, his left hand, and the misspelled words appeared at the bottom of the screen.

Why dont u take yor shirt off sexxy.

Susanna recoiled from the computer as if stung, remembering the webcam. The little dot in the top center of the laptop. A device she had never used, assuming that she would have to do something, maybe go into settings, even to turn the thing on. She reached behind her and grabbed the first thing that came to hand, the scarf she had been wearing when she arrived home. She flung it over the computer, capturing the webcam in its folds as she might capture a Christmas beetle to stop it tangling in her hair. Behind the drape of the red scarf she could see the man working on his fully erect penis. She put her hand to her chest, noticed the wild beat of her heart and tried to calm it with deep regular breaths.

There were new words on the bottom of the screen. She could

see a few of them and it was the words that lured her to lift the edge of the scarf. If she left it draped over the top part of the computer she would be free to watch and not be seen. There was some comfort in this. She adjusted the fabric and concentrated on the words.

Have you gone drling Come back you were soooo hot

She thought about it. She reached out for the keyboard, shy Susanna who could never be drawn into a conversation. She found her fingers trembling a little on the keys.

I am still here. I am watching.

your camera drpped out. His one-handed jumbled conversation. *turn yr camera back on u so hot*

And Susanna, calmer now: *I will watch but you can't see me.*

ok. do u like what you c

I can't see the bottom of your hand, I can't see all of you

Tell me wht u can c hottie. say those drty words

I can see your cock. A little blush, a little wave of adrenaline racing along her veins. *I can see the head of your cock and the shaft and some of your hand. I can see your nipples, you have dark nipples. I can see your hairy chest but the camera stops short of your neck. I can't see your balls.*

u want to c my balls?

I am curious. I have only seen one man's balls

tell me what his balls r like

She typed quickly and with a growing confidence. She felt the rise of her own pleasure. It was like that first time, the quick insistence of her lust rearing suddenly, obliterating her shyness as it warmed her loins.

Smooth. Almost hairless, tight, and with a little dark line running down the length of them. When he came they tightened in my mouth. I liked that. That physical expression of his love. The way his balls tightened and his hand on his cock quickened and then the sight of it, the thick semen spraying up onto his stomach.

She was certain she had conjured it. His orgasm coincided perfectly with her words. She watched as the precome leaked down over his fingers and suddenly it was more than that, ejaculate spurting higher than she expected, splattering up onto his chest, spraying pearly drops onto his tight black nipples. The little aftershocks, the dying spurts leaking down the length of his still-hard shaft. She watched, shifting in her chair, uncomfortable in her state of arousal. The screen dipped to black, the connection gone. Her love's namesake disappeared forever. Then, before she had time to reach out and close the computer the words, those fateful words flaring up onto the screen.

Another partner is waiting for you. Would you like to play?

Her clitoris hummed, her own juices had begun to leak out from between the lips that were already swollen with excitement. The words flashed in a rhythm that she could easily settle into.

Would you like to play? Would you like to play?

Susanna checked that her scarf was still securely fixed over her webcam. She reached out to the keyboard and tapped lightly with her index finger. Yes. *Yes.* She did want to play.

MEET ME AT THE SPANISH STEPS

Lucy Felthouse

Meet me at the Spanish Steps, the text said. It also specified a day and time. The following day, at 1:00 p.m.

A few seconds later, my phone bleeped again.

I'll text you in the morning and let you know what I'm wearing. Will you do the same?

I replied in the affirmative. Although I knew what he looked like, our knowing what the other was wearing would help us to find each other in the no doubt huge crowds surrounding the famous tourist attraction. I was glad, because there was no way I wanted to miss out on meeting up with him. My sanity—and libido—were riding on it.

Since I'd been working on the campsite on the outskirts of Rome, I'd been doing my best to learn Italian, and I was improving rapidly. But it would be some time before I progressed to learning the words and phrases necessary for getting what I wanted in the bedroom. As a result, my kinky cravings went unfulfilled, and although I was having the odd fuck here and there with other staff on the site and the occasional Italian, I was desperate to have sex the way I really wanted it. Needed it. I couldn't ask the English-speaking staff that I went to bed with, because I still had to face them day after day. And with six months left on my contract, the last thing I needed were rumors going around about my unusual sexual appetite.

Which is why I'd turned to the Internet. I found William through a website for Brits living abroad, and from the very beginning I'd been clear that I was looking for sex, rather than love, and that I had particular tastes that I wanted him to cater to. He was more than willing to scratch those specific itches and we went from exchanging emails to text messages, to eventually arranging to meet.

The following morning, I dressed with care, and paid special attention to my hair and makeup. The funny part was, I was paying attention to make sure my clothes were easy to remove, my hair was easily tidied if it got messed up, and my makeup wouldn't smudge. After ensuring my bag contained the all-important condoms, tissues and pepper spray—a girl can never be too careful—I hit the road.

By the time I emerged from Spagna Metro station, I was ready and raring to go. I was a little nervous, but that was more down to the risk that despite all his assurances, William wouldn't be able to give me what I so desperately needed. I really didn't want to be left high and dry. I buried my misgivings deep inside my subconscious and mentally kept my fingers crossed that they wouldn't come to fruition. Then, after taking a quick peek in the pocket-sized mirror I always carried, I walked along the narrow alley leading from the Metro station out to the *piazza* at the bottom of the Spanish Steps.

I was quickly enveloped by the crowds, and I started to worry that in spite of William and I sharing details of our attire, we wouldn't find each other. A little while later, I realized my worries had been unfounded. I spotted him leaning against the wall of Babington's Tea Room, wearing exactly what he'd said he would, and a huge smile besides. Grinning back, I shoved my way past meandering tourists and finally reached him.

"Hi, Darby," he said, stepping forward to shake my hand— very British—then releasing it after the prerequisite amount of time.

"Hi," I responded, trying to subtly check him out. We'd exchanged photos, but they never really did a person justice, nor did they really give a clue as to whether you'd fancy someone or not. And, desperate as I was to drag a fellow English speaker to bed and make my erotic demands, there was no way that was going to happen if I wasn't actually attracted to him. I wasn't that desperate.

He held out his arm, and I took it, as he told me, "I thought we'd go into Babington's, if that's all right with you. Do you know the history of the place?"

I nodded. I was somewhat of a history buff; therefore I was well aware of the fact that the tea rooms had been founded by two British ladies, one of whom was from my home county, Derbyshire. I appreciated his attention to detail, though, and considered this a point in his favor.

A little while later, we were enjoying a delicious cream tea and the conversation was coming along well. William was witty and intelligent as well as attractive, and it was soon obvious to me that there was a spark between us. Once I realized it, I was suddenly desperate to get out of there and go somewhere more private.

"Well," I said, draining my dainty teacup and putting it carefully back on its saucer, "that was delicious. It's been wonderful to have a taste of English after a few months out here."

William raised an eyebrow. I met his gaze boldly, and moved

my arms so they squeezed my ample breasts together, creating a very impressive cleavage in my low-cut top.

He coughed. "Well, Darby, I have to say I'm inclined to agree." Looking around us, evidently to see if anyone was in earshot, he leaned toward me and continued, "But I'd really like to have a real taste of English, if you're so inclined."

His gaze lingered on my tits then slowly raked back up to my face. His eyes were full of mischief and intent. A rush of lust zipped to my pussy. I broke eye contact, only to hurriedly scramble inside my bag for my purse so I could pay the bill and get the hell out of there.

That was obviously all the answer William needed. He grasped my wrist, slightly harder than necessary—clearly hinting that he was capable of catering to my needs—and murmured, "Don't worry about that. Go and wait outside while I pay. You're looking a little hot."

I gave him a mock scowl—he knew damn well why I was feeling hot—but did as he said. I had just a couple of minutes to people watch before he was at my side once more.

"Shall we?" he said, holding out his arm once more.

I took it. "Where are we going?"

He knew I lived and worked on the outskirts of the city, but I had no idea where he lived. I hoped it was close. The anticipation of what we were about to do was making hormones pump through my body at a rapid pace, and as my clit swelled, every single step became torture and pleasure rolled into one.

"Not far," he responded, leading me back toward the Metro station. Instead of walking down the long corridor to the platforms—which was lined with people selling fake designer goods, eager to catch tourists and commuters alike—he veered off to the right and into an area which held lifts and a staircase.

I frowned, wondering what was up from here. It was a public

access area, so it obviously didn't lead to any private dwellings or premises. Seconds later, the lift pinged its arrival, and, always the gentleman, William indicated I should go ahead of him. As soon as the doors closed—mercifully we hadn't been joined by anyone else—he was upon me.

His hands grabbed my hips and pushed me against the grubby, graffiti-covered metal wall of the lift. Pinning me there with his entire body—and I certainly didn't miss the fact that there was an eager erection pressing into my stomach—he leaned down to kiss me. Only it wasn't just any kiss. It was the kiss I'd been craving for months. It was rough, possessive and so erotic that I was glad he was holding me up, otherwise my knees probably would have given out.

William's agile tongue continued to plunder my mouth until the lift slowed to a stop. Instantly, he stepped away from me. As soon as the doors opened, he grabbed my hand and all but marched out, pulling me breathless and gaping behind him. I barely had time to register that we were now at the square at the top of the Spanish Steps before I was led quickly past the artists and flower sellers, then past the church and down the street opposite.

After a few twists and turns, I quickly lost my bearings, then began to wonder how far "not far" was. Before I had time to ask, we stopped in front of a nondescript-looking building. William released my hand, dug in his pocket and produced some keys. He slotted the relevant one into the lock, and milliseconds later was ushering me into the gloomy hallway. He then made sure the outside door was properly closed before starting to climb the staircase in front of him.

He said nothing, so I merely followed in silence up two flights, before coming to a stop as William unlocked his apartment door.

Once inside, I half expected him to pin me against the door and kiss me breathless like he had in the lift. Instead, he pointed to a door on the far side of the room, and said, "Go in there. Take off all of your clothes, put them neatly on the chair. Then bend over the bed and wait for me."

I gave a small nod, then immediately moved to do his bidding. My blood thundered through my veins, and my pussy grew ever slicker. My clit was a veritable time bomb, needing but the briefest touch to make it explode. Entering the bedroom, I closed the door behind me and removed my clothes quickly, dropping them and my bag onto the chair as he'd requested.

Then I moved over to the bed, placed my palms on the mattress and bent over. As my ass pointed rudely into the air, I felt a trickle of my pussy juices slide down and coat my inner thighs. By now, I was in no doubt that William would coax lots more juices out of me, and a great many orgasms. My entire body buzzed with anticipation. Fortunately, I didn't have to wait too much longer for my encounter to begin.

I closed my eyes as I heard the door open. It hadn't been part of William's orders, but I always felt everything so much more keenly when I was deprived of my sight. It also seemed to make my hearing sharper, and I used that benefit to try and work out what he was doing.

A soft click as he closed the bedroom door. Clothes brushing against one another as he crossed the room. More fabric sounds, and a *zzzip* as he undid his jeans. The soft *thwap* as each garment hit the floor. Movement. The opening...then the closing of a drawer. The unmistakable and incredibly erotic sound of...

He was right behind me. There was silence, but somehow I could sense him, and I even fancied I could feel the heat of his body permeating my naked skin.

"Good," he said quietly, reaching out a hand to stroke my

behind, "you've followed my directions exactly. Unfortunately for you, though, even good girls get punished."

My heart rate increased at his words. I knew what he held in his free hand, and I was desperate to feel it on my flesh. I remained silent, waiting. Willing him to get on with it. To bring me to the earth-shattering climax I so needed.

I was so deep inside my own head, examining my wants and needs, that the first strike of the leather paddle actually took me by surprise. I couldn't stop the yelp that burst from my lips, but I didn't move. Proudly, I remained bent over the bed, my ass remaining resolutely elevated and waiting for the next hit. Already, the sting and the heat were morphing into something much more pleasurable, and my clit and vulva swelled. If William took the time to look, I was sure he would be presented with an incredibly lewd sight. I hoped he wouldn't, though. Not yet. If he peeked now, he might not be able to resist thrusting his cock between my pouting labia and into my eager cunt. I wanted it, of course, but I could get straight sex anywhere.

First, I needed to have my kinky desires sated. And as the second strike landed on my eager buttocks, I thanked the inventor of the Internet for enabling me to find someone willing to do it, even though I was over a thousand miles from home with only a basic grip of the native language. I made no sound this time, merely sucking in a breath through my nostrils and enjoying the rush of endorphins that coursed through my bloodstream. My pussy throbbed. By the time William got around to fucking me, I'd probably have wetness running down to my ankles.

I wiggled my ass enticingly, inviting the next blow. My coquettishness obviously annoyed William, as he picked up his pace. Smacks three, four and five came in rapid succession, and I barely had a chance to absorb the feelings from each before the next one arrived. Despite this, he'd taken great care to ensure that he was covering different parts of my ass and even the tops of my thighs, so by the time he'd completed the round of punishment—fifteen spanks—the entire area was burning. You could have fried an egg on my ass.

I slumped down a little, resting my forehead on the bed, my chest heaving. I couldn't remember the last time I'd felt so incredibly horny. My cunt was so ready that I fancied it was gaping, ready to gobble the next cock that came within fucking distance, and my clit ached, almost to the point of pain.

I was on the knife-edge of climax, so when I heard the opening and closing of a drawer, the tearing of a wrapper and the snap of rubber, I quickly pushed myself back up on my arms, presenting my reddened ass to him once more. William stroked his finger along my vulva and finding me soaked, bothered with no further foreplay. With one hand he aimed his cockhead at my entrance, and with the other he gripped my asscheek.

He slid inside me to the hilt—I was so wet that he met with zero resistance—and I stretched to accommodate him. I hadn't seen what my fellow Brit had to offer in the trouser department, but now that his cock was buried inside me, I knew he was blessed. Not ridiculously so, but enough to please any woman. Or man, for that matter.

I was wound so tight that I was convinced a mere puff of air against my clit would send me reeling into orgasm. But William was nowhere near as gentle as that. He began to thrust inside my saturated cunt, and the room was filled with a rude sucking sound that would have bordered on embarrassing if I hadn't been so damn horny and desperate to come. He increased his pace, shoving inside me forcefully, his fingertips digging into my abused buttocks, sending fresh zings of pleasure/pain to my pussy.

His grunts and moans added to the sucking sounds, and I knew it wouldn't be long before he came. The paddling he'd given me had obviously turned him on massively, too. I got my answer in kind when he reached around my hip, slipped his hand between my legs and pinched my clit as he continued to fuck me with jerky, shallow thrusts.

That was all it took. My clit was like an overfilled balloon, bursting at the tiniest provocation. I gripped the bedspread until my knuckles turned white, my cunt spasming wildly around William's cock as wave after wave of excruciating pleasure slammed into my body. I almost passed out with the sensation, it was so intense. I shook my head dazedly, determined to stay coherent enough to enjoy the thing I'd been craving for so long.

I was vaguely aware of William's grunted expletives and the twitches of his shaft as he emptied his own release inside me. But to be honest, I didn't really care. He wasn't my boyfriend. He was barely even a lover. He was just a fuck. I chastised myself. I should be nicer to him, I decided, because although he was just a fuck, he was a damn good one. And he was hopefully going to be a frequent one that would be willing to scratch my kinky itches until my season at the campsite was up.

Because the spanking had just been the beginning. I had many more bedroom fetishes I liked to indulge in, and, as William pulled out and dragged me onto the bed with him, his cock already reawakening, I knew he was the perfect candidate to play my kinky games.

For the next six months, anyway.

DIRECTOR LADY

Anika Ray

He said he was twenty-one, but he was probably younger. With a body like a coil of rope, lean and tanned and throbbing. I told him to undress in the middle of the floor, and he looked at me with the terrible sadness of someone who'd been betrayed.

I swallowed and in a flash of heat fell down, melted, a mess of legs and the boy at the copier and the boy at the desk and the boy between my legs at the desk—just dreams. The dreams all came up, and I pushed through them.

"Take your clothes off," I said, like it was suddenly important to me personally. Outside the girl who handled the casting was checking names against a list, but I was thinking only about this one man. Here. Now.

The other girl didn't see it, his dropping green eyes and long brown brow. She was leaning against the exposed brick wall entirely nude with one long leg crossed over the other. Her pussy was shaved; her hair was shiny and ironed. She was picking at her nails and didn't even look up as we did the screen test.

"We're picking a new star for you, Cherry," I said. She was a redhead. The last guy who'd come in, she'd devoured him with her eyes and sent him home.

"He fucks like a machine," she'd yawned, bored, looking at us over her gleaming wet ass. "A dumb one."

So we'd gotten her a fresh machine. He came out of his clothes like it was a dance, missing a button and kicking at his woolen pants. He had thick lines of muscle in his hips, and I bit down on my lips.

Cherry kept on picking at her nails. Dead skin hit the floor.

"Start by licking her pussy," I said. Dragging, dropping, he went toward her. A boy in a man's body; knelt down, apologetic.

"Ma'am…" and Cherry, bitch that she was, just canted one knee a little away from the other. Making him work for it.

Soft little velvet cat's tongue. I watched it slide between Cherry's neatly trimmed artificial-looking lips, like the lips of a suction machine, not human at all. Back and forth. Cherry put one hand on the wall, another on his head like giving a benediction. Her eyes stared straight ahead as her little hips rode his head. He jerked back and forth, trying to make her moan. She closed her eyes in infinite patience.

"Yeah, that's right," she said, on an exhaled breath.

"Put your fingers inside her," I said, feeling those little fingers on me, his hands poking at the insides of my thighs, that little flickering tongue stabbing. One long, narrow finger went into Cherry, between the shaved pussy lips, deep into the inside part that no one ever saw, the only part of Cherry that no one ever saw.

She rocked back and forth on her heels. He twisted his wrist, corkscrew; Cherry bent her knees until she was almost sitting on his shoulders, and he put his free hand on her stomach. *Feel it here, baby, right here*…that hand pushing down as the other came up from within.

Camera whirring. It was hot, we were all sweating under the lights as Cherry lay down, spread her legs for the camera. The boy with his questioning green eyes lay down beside her as if he didn't know what to do, and suddenly it became vitally important that he know the next move.

The candles were too long in their silver holders. His hands were inside her from behind, up to the palm, he was twisting and grinding his fingers against her, inside her, trying to work her.

She probably didn't feel a thing.

"Try something bigger," I said, and Cherry stared, hard, like she'd fallen down. And he put out his hand and found the silver candlestick, wrapped with nubs of waxy melt, put it in his soft pillow of a mouth.

"That?" asked Cherry on her side in front of him, looking over her shoulder. "I..." But it was too late, the wet gleaming stick came up between her legs and one hand came around her flat drum stomach, reached down, parted her wet, brown pussy lips even as the other brought the stick up, wet it in her juices, eased it in.

"Go in deep," I said, tense, on the edge.

"Ugh," Cherry said, but the boy's hands held her, becoming more sure, more certain, and inch by inch he worked that big round silver stick into Cherry's much-used twat, until her hips were moving back and forth like a flag in a wind.

"Ask her how it feels," I shouted at him, voice rising at the end like it was a question.

"How does that feel?" asked the boy. His voice was like sandpaper on wood, roughing up the edges. The stick came in and out like a song and Cherry tapped the rhythm, eyes closed, hand on the wooden floor. Camera came in close.

"Oh, this is good, this is good," whispered the grip, lost.

"Feels good," said Cherry, rolling, gasping, fucking the

candlestick with her matron's unused hips, pussy lips eating the silver and spitting it out, polished, pearled.

"Keep going," I said, as Cherry whispered, cried, closed her eyes tight and grabbed on to the rug. She rolled forward and from behind the boy's cock dove—tight, thick, ready. A young man's cock. God, Cherry was going to get that cock in a minute, the boy was looking at her gasping pussy with fascination. I knew what it must feel like, from the inside; that soft, tight ring of vaginal muscle and the long smooth inward slide.

After the first stroke it was easy.

"Come on, come on, fuck her," I whispered, tight, straining against my chair. "Come on, she's ready, just..."

And the boy looked up. Lightning shivered in his eyes.

"Do it to her," I moaned, leaning all the way forward. I don't know how it happened, the rug was against my back, and suddenly I was next to them.

"Put your cock here," I said, pointing at Cherry's rhythmic, stroking pussy. But I fell, and the boy loomed over me. "Your cock," I tried to tell him. I could see it, rising, fast, and then his bright eyes pierced me; Cherry was gasping and covered with sweat beside me.

"I came," she said with wonder, the candlestick between her thighs.

"But," I gasped, dissatisfied, "he didn't do it right."

"How?" asked Cherry, looking at me. "How?"

"He didn't put his cock into you, Cherry, the viewers won't like it..." The smell and shadow fell over me first, and then I felt the bone against my bones.

"Director lady," he said, and I grasped his elbows to say, *Hold on, we can still make it work,* but my legs came apart and with one hand he raised my skirt; the other spread me open like he'd done with Cherry.

The first is always the hardest. The ring of muscle, the pop, the head coming home. His eyes went blank above me, lost in pleasure.

"Oh, you poor baby," I said, soft, low, as my hips gave him the pleasure he needed, and the cameras came in.

Cherry said it to him: "Slow, slow, she likes it slow," and I felt the drag and lisp of a cock grating against bottom. I grasped his elbows and opened my legs and he pushed in deeper, deeper.

"Don't move," said Cherry, but the boy wouldn't listen, he couldn't keep still.

"Ugh," he groaned, slamming his hips into me twice, three times, each time nailing a note up inside me, letting the tension knot and build; I saw his lost green gaze, then his eyes closed, he was lost in me.

I took him into me, I rocked against him; Cherry pushed eagerly against us both.

Time opened, suspended, his cock caught against my inside; I sealed him into my hips, pumped up, unraveled.

Hard, horsey breathing. Mine and Cherry's.

The boy's soft, limp dick slid out of me. He looked down, fearful, cautious.

"Ma'am," he said, suddenly afraid, apologetic. I caressed the warm muscles of his hard ass, the dents in his back. "I..."

Rough voice.

I lay on the rug savoring it, as the cameras cooled down.

BEING HIS BITCH

Janine Ashbless

The theme for the Club Night this month was "The Pet Show." There was no way that Dev and I were going to miss this one, and we put a lot of effort into my costume—or rather, lack of costume, since it was nearly all body paint. I picked the color scheme based on a boxer dog that lives down our street: cream belly and chest, but a beautiful dark brindle all over the back and legs and face. I had my hair cut short and elfin and made a pair of dog ears in velvety faux fur that sat atop my head, half-pricked and endearingly floppy. Dev did the paintwork himself, using a skin-friendly, grease-free ink; he's in graphic design, and he loves to get his art kit out when he has an excuse to do something properly creative.

The airbrushing took a couple of hours, there were so many layers. "It ought to last out the night, unless you rub it off," he said. But I wasn't making any promises.

To finish off my costume, we had a dog collar—a broad greyhound one that made me hold my head up, with a dog tag dangling from it—and a chain leash with a leather loop. Engraved on the disc was the legend "Naughty Little Bitch." We could've got that done discreetly ourselves, using one of those machines you find in pet stores, but Dev made me go into the engraver's shop and order it in person from the man behind the counter. The guy gave me one hell of a look but didn't ask any questions, and I emerged from the shop with my panties so wet and my legs so wobbly that I could hardly walk straight.

"All done?" Dev asked.

"Yes," I whispered, leaning my head against his chest.

He knew what that meant. Taking the disc from me with one hand, he put the other on my ass and gave me a squeeze and a pat. "Good girl." I whimpered and rubbed up against him, but he just chuckled. "Save it for Saturday night."

By Saturday I was strung out on anticipation and so inflamed with arousal that Dev had to order me to stop touching myself as we drove into the city. I shed my coat in the cloakroom with a feeling of profound relief.

Dev was wearing his favorite club costume: a kilt of thick industrial rubber, New Rock boots, and a steampunk top hat and goggles. He looked so good in that gear that I wanted to suck his cock already. I could see that quite a few people had turned up in some version of Furry costume, and I was sure I'd be a lot more comfortable than all of them in the heat of the rooms upstairs, but comfort wasn't what it was all about, here.

Dev clipped the leash to my collar and used it to pull me to him and plant a kiss on my lips, all slippery, possessive tongue, reminding me where my focus lay for the evening. "Ready?"

"Yes." Already people were checking me out, there in the lobby. I was aware of grins and raised eyebrows and nods. Under my paint I was naked and shaved as smooth as silk. I looked respectable from a distance but incredibly naughty close up, and that made my nipples stand out like switches ready to be flicked.

"I love you, Rosie," he growled. "So fucking much. You're so beautiful." Then he tugged the chain. "Heel, bitch."

We ascended the stairs slowly, morphing into character with every step, his pace proud and easy, my obedient place at his side and one step behind. Playing this particular game is, for me, the ultimate in intimacy. Playing it in public for the first time was taking our trust in one another to a whole new level.

We went into the bar first and queued so that Dev could order drinks—bottled beer for him, bottled water for me. As soon as he stopped walking I sank to my knees by his leg, waiting patiently as a good dog should. We had considered my staying on hands and knees throughout the night but had decided it would be irritatingly slow to move around, not to mention painful for me and not in a good way. Going to dog height when we were stationary seemed the best compromise.

"Hello Dev." Black leather chaps loomed over me. It was Bill, a club friend and someone we had played with before, but I didn't try to greet him. I was being a mute animal, after all. "Nice dog you've got there."

"Thank you."

"What's her name?"

"Princess."

"May I stroke her?" Etiquette is everything at the club. People are scrupulously respectful of boundaries: without that the whole thing would fall apart.

"Go ahead. She likes having her chest rubbed." Dev turned away slightly to give his order to the barman, and Bill stooped to scratch me gently behind the ears—my real ears.

I opened my mouth, panting a little and leaning into the caress. It was stuffy down here among the forest of legs. I could smell leather and spilt beer. The front of my admirer's pants was tented by a bulge, but that didn't mean anything in particular: most of the guys here walk round with a semi the whole night, and I can't speak for all the girls, but my pussy is open and juicy and fluttering from the moment we walk in. Bill crouched to caress the smooth cream blaze of my chest, stroking my breasts, and I shut my eyes in pleasure, pushing those orbs up into his hand. *I'm a dog. Anybody may stroke me, so long as my master gives permission. Anybody.*

"Good girl, Princess," he murmured. His fingers flicked my pert nipples. "You like that, don't you?"

I didn't answer, but as Dev turned back to us and Bill stood to talk to my owner once more, I caught the tips of his fingers with my tongue and licked them, and he laughed.

Carrying both drinks, Dev walked me though the rooms of the club—the dance floor, the theatre, the playroom where the keenest members were already warming up with floggers and paddles on the various pieces of equipment—and into the lounge. This has comfortable chairs and cushions, and there were plenty of people standing and sitting about, talking and showing off their costumes. I couldn't help looking furtively around, though my attention was supposed to be on Dev. They looked so beautiful, in their way. Not everyone had stuck to the Pet Show theme; it wasn't compulsory, so long as you wore something fetish. But many had. Cats and dogs mostly, though there was one woman in full pony-girl tack, including a small cart, and I've no idea how she and her driver had managed to get that up the stairs. A couple of kittens stopped their tussling to hiss at me as I walked past, and I rose to the challenge and barked excitedly in response, causing Dev to tow me away by my collar. As we retreated to the far side of the room, I saw one kitten pin the other and begin to give her a good licking.

Being surrounded by others with the calling to kink made my

heart swell with awe and my sex ache. I could feel my libido slip free of its constraints and start to soar.

We met another couple we knew quite well. Annie, normally a carefully preened platinum blonde, was all in Dalmatian spots tonight, and she carried a rag rope between her teeth. As our two owners stood and watched, Annie and I had a tug-of-war game with the rope on hands and knees, jumping on each other and mouthing excitedly as we wrestled for the toy. That was fun: naughty fun, what with hands and mouths and bare bodies rubbing all over each other, but just plain childish fun too. There is such a lack of inhibition in being a dog, a simple innocence that still has room for sex. Annie nipped me on the ass until I squealed and rolled over in submission, surrendering her prize.

Annie's owner took her away toward the bar, the rope held triumphantly in her mouth, as I sat up panting. At that moment another dog came bowling in on all fours, his leash flying behind him. He bounced up and down around me, tongue lolling and ears flopping wildly, while I tried to stifle my giggles. Unlike me, he wore a tail: a stiff curl that rose from the butt-plug planted between his ass cheeks and waved with every step. I recognized him too; he was a well-known TV comedian. We sometimes get famous faces here, but discretion is also part of the rigid etiquette. Spinning top to tail, he made a show of sniffing my behind. I obliged, as dogs do, standing foursquare and then nudging his flank with my nose. Underneath the pale skin of his belly, his latex codpiece was stretched by his jutting stiffy. I stooped and gave the shiny rubber a little lick—just before Dev pulled me away.

"Get off!" he ordered, amused. "You filthy dogs!"

The comedian grinned, panting—and then bounded away as a woman rushed up waving a rolled-up newspaper. "Fido!" she snapped, grabbing his leash and swatting his ass good and hard.

He howled in happy self-pity. She looked over her shoulder at Dev. "I'm so sorry! Has he been bothering your bitch? He's such a bad dog: he won't obey a word I say!"

"No problem," grinned Dev. "Just keep him away from the cats."

The naughty dog decided that sounded like a great idea and, spotting the pretty kittens on the far side of the room, set off determinedly toward them, yipping and towing his mistress. I had to cover my mouth with my hand to hide my giggles.

"Okay," said Dev. "I think we need to calm down."

I tried to look contrite as he led me to a chair in a corner. Sitting, he stretched his legs out in front of him and crossed his ankles. I took up my customary position straddling his shins, my head on his lap. I love Dev, but when I'm being Princess I love him even more, with a dog's unstinting trust and devotion. My pussy rested comfortably on the jut of his booted foot, my bare ass pointing at the world. Dev sipped his beer and watched me, his gaze sliding over the curves of my shoulders and waist and butt, over my spread thighs.

"Thirsty?"

I nodded. There was no rule against me talking, but silence helped me feel in character. Dev held the plastic glass of water to the level of my mouth and I lapped at it, grateful despite my awkwardness.

"You enjoying yourself, Princess?"

I smiled, my eyebrows telegraphing how much wicked fun I was having, and wriggled my bottom against the upper of his boot. The leather felt cool against my warm, wet pussy.

"Dirty little bitch," he murmured, pressing up into the concavity of my sex as his fingers tickled my neck and jaw. A chrome boot stud rubbed my clit, and I sighed with pleasure. "You would have let that bad dog lick your ass, wouldn't you?"

I shrugged, teasing.

"You'd have let him mount you, dirty little bitch." His fingers stroked my throat, making me groan. I could feel the wet I was leaving on his polished leather.

Yes, maybe I would have. It's hard to think ahead when you're a dog; that's the master's job. I wasn't feeling at all responsible right now: I was aroused and completely surrendered to Dev's caressing fingers and pressing boot. Part of me was aware of the room around me, but only as a setting and a witness to my unashamed pleasure.

"Maybe I should find you a good stud dog."

Heat flooded my cunt, and I opened my eyes wide in alarm.

"We can probably do better than that silly mongrel." Dev set aside the drinks and reached to fondle my breasts. "What do you think, Princess?"

"Oh," I said, as he tugged my nipples, rolling and pinching them between his fingers. Hot lashes of sensation ran all the way down from his fingertips to my clit.

"Yes, I think that's a very good idea. A nice big stud dog to mate with my horny little bitch."

I met his gaze, my trepidation undisguised. We'd played with other people at the club, sure: I'd been spanked and scratched, groped and tickled. But that was all. It had never gone all the way. The thought of Dev picking someone to fuck me...

It made me burn and squirm and recoil and grind my hips.

"Which one shall I choose?" he whispered, sending shivers all over my painted skin. My heart was beating so hard he must have been able to feel it against his knee. "Something with a good pedigree. Something strong and fit and eager. With a nice big cock and fat, heavy balls. Something..." He lifted his face, looking out into the room. "What do you think?"

I craned my neck to see.

Oh, *fuck*. It was Mistress Freda and her sub, Victor.

That thought was nearly enough to make me come there and then; a quivering spasm ran through me. Freda and Victor were a couple I'd had a crush on since we joined the club. So did everyone else, I think. They stand out in this crowd because they're black, but those two would stand out anywhere. They're both really tall and fiercely beautiful, and this night Freda was wearing a tight, boned pastiche of traditional hunting habit: a precariously low-cut red jacket and a miniature hat and veil, and shiny black boots with heels that could stake a vampire. Her long corn-rowed hair hung down her back in cords as tight and cruel as the lashes of a cat-o'-nine-tails. There was a riding crop holstered at her hip, and we were under no illusions that she knew how to use it. I've heard she's some sort of scary corporate lawyer.

I've no idea what Victor does for a day job, but he's built with the sort of hyper-real muscles you only see on sportsmen and in rap videos, and all of it was on show that night. His dress consisted mostly of leather strapping: one of those chest harnesses people put on bull terriers and mastiffs, with the legend "REX" printed down the breastbone, and a set of tack and metal rings around his ass and cock and balls that fully displayed his vital parts, flushed and swollen and ready. A glans-ring completed the "pet" theme: a chain led from it to Freda's elegant, nonchalant fingers.

"Whoa!" I moaned, forgetting myself. Dev chuckled.

It's not like we know Freda and Victor to talk to. She's a really haughty domme, and though she will deign to punish other people's subs sometimes, she plays too rough for most. I like a little recreational spanking, but they're in another league altogether. Victor likes *serious* pain. When the Club Night theme was "Pirates," she'd tied him to a ship's wheel and whipped his back and ass raw with a leather strap, and he'd taken it without complaint. Groaned, sweated, clenched his teeth, yes— but taken it, and then got down to kiss her toes afterward and thanked her profusely.

"Hmm?" said Dev pointedly. "Would you like that, Princess?"

I tore my gaze from the other couple to meet his, biting my lip. My face was burning, my pussy melting. But I didn't say anything. I desperately wanted him to make the decision. He was the master, not me.

Dev lifted one eyebrow, and I felt his legs shift beneath me. "Sit, girl."

I moved back to sit on my heels, my heart pounding. He stood slowly, watching me with a critical eye.

"Legs open."

Obediently I spread my thighs.

"Now—stay." He let the chain leash slip from his hand to hang down between my outthrust breasts. The loop handle brushed my bare and sensitized mons, and I quivered inside. I watched him stroll away toward Mistress Freda, and I swallowed hard, trying to work moisture back into my nervous mouth. It all seemed to have drained down to my sex, which felt swollen and heavy.

This is real. Oh, god—he's really going to ask. I'm a good dog. He'll look after me. I am doing as my master wants. I'm a good good dog.

He spoke to her. I watched the confident tilt of his shoulders and the easy nod of his head, gesturing back at me. I couldn't help admiring the sweep of his long kilt and the dull gleam of the rubber. Victor—or Rex—was kneeling quietly at his mistress's side, his neck turned so that he could look up at her with calm devotion. The light glistened on his muscled chest: he was a

Rottweiler among toy poodles. When she glanced over at me, a sharp sweet pain contracted inside my belly. I dropped my gaze to the floorboards, too shy to meet hers.

Oh, god. They were coming over. All three of them.

"Here she is," said Dev. How could he sound so calm?

"Hh," she grunted. "Kneel up straight." Obediently I hauled my ass clear of my heels. The floorboards felt hard beneath my knees. She hunkered down directly in front of me, and a casual tug upon the cock-chain of her pet brought him to his knees at her side. My vision was blurred, but I could see the morello cherry glisten of her lips and the swing and bob of his turgid length. She smelled expensive and wonderful. Slipping a hand between my parted thighs, she explored my pussy. Her nails were frighteningly long, but she was delicate, for which I was grateful as her fingers slithered over my swollen folds, paddling in the slick juiciness within. I was so wet that it was seeping down the insides of my legs. When she stroked my clit with one fingertip, a charge shot through me, and I couldn't help whimpering.

"Yes, I think you're right: your bitch *is* in heat." Withdrawing her hand, Freda held it up, glistening with my wetness. Her nails were painted in red-and-black tiger stripes. Apex predator. "Luckily for her I have the solution here."

Victor sniffed her proffered fingers, then licked them slowly and lovingly. I could feel my thighs starting to shake.

"What do you think, Rex?" she purred. We all looked at him. His answer was a great big piratical grin aimed straight at me. My heart crashed wildly. I turned to Dev for reassurance, cuddling up to his leg.

"She's a bit nervous, I'm afraid." He cupped my throat with one hand and fondled my tit with the other.

"Young bitches often are, at first." Freda's smirk was wicked.

"She'll learn to love it. Shall we?"

"Come on, Princess." Dev urged me to my feet and led me to the center of the room. There's a broad bench there, padded in red leatherette: a seat sometimes, but often a stage for whatever club members choose to display in public. I heard the room grow quieter as I climbed upon it, onto hands and knees, and Dev coaxed my thighs a little apart and my head up like I was Best of Breed at Crufts Dog Show.

Oh, god. He's going to do it to me in public. They can all see my pussy now.

"My dirty little bitch," he murmured hoarsely, stooping to rub his face against mine. "Oh you dirty girl, you wonderful dirty girl."

I licked his lips.

Dev held my leash loosely as Freda led her pet round to my head. Standing, his cock was on a level with my mouth. His pubic hair was shaved down to a tight stubble, and his genitals, in their harness and rings, looked magnificent.

"Lick him," ordered Freda, tugging his cock on its chain and bringing him a step closer, right to my lips.

I was aware of people gathering around us to watch.

He had a truly beautiful cock, strong and straight and smooth, framed against thighs and a stomach like polished walnut. The glans-ring yanked it to full vertical, allowing me unrestricted access to the underside of the shaft and to his balls. That's where I started licking him. My mouth wasn't dry any more, but watering with hunger. He tasted good too—completely different from Dev, but just as yummy: masculine and musky with a hint of sandalwood soap. I could feel the heat surge through his shaft as I licked, filling it. He grunted in appreciation and pressed forward, rubbing his cock all over my face, hefting his scrotum so I could lick that too. I wasn't sucking tonight: dogs don't suck. I was all tongue as I worked my way from that big pouch hanging below, right up to the tip of his glans where a clear teardrop of pre-cum awaited me.

"Step back," said Freda, as it burned on my pouting lips. Victor shifted out of my reach, and she unclipped the chain from his glans-ring. The angle of his thick shaft didn't drop at all; he was at full and straining erection now. I heard a sigh of anticipation run through the circle around us. Dev ran his fingers down my spine. Reaching into the cleft of her awesome cleavage, Freda extracted a condom. She tore the wrapper open with her teeth, then skinned it onto her pet with swift grace and something near a flourish. Patting him on the ass, she instructed, "Take her, Rex."

He walked round behind me, harness jingling with each step. The crowd shifted, following him with their eyes, but I looked up at Dev. He cupped my chin in his hand. His eyes were shining, his throat glossed with perspiration. "Good girl."

I expected Victor to mount me straight away, but he put his big hands on my butt-cheeks and spread them. I knew my smooth pink crack and my flushed pussy were completely open to him. Then he took me by surprise, because he stooped and licked me, all the way up from my clit to my anus. I squealed and he did it again, burrowing his face in hard, sucking my swollen sex-lips, lapping and licking and slurping until I was dizzy with shock, then squirming his tongue into the tight clench of my back entrance. I'm a screamer: I can't keep quiet. I certainly wasn't quiet here. My squeals and cries rose like a musical scale. I arched my back and threw my head up and down. Yet in the middle of all that noise and chaos I felt completely safe, because Dev was holding my collar and keeping an eye on every move Victor made.

Only when he'd tasted me and opened me thoroughly did my

big stud dog kneel up behind me on the leatherette and slap his cock against my pussy. I sank my shoulders down, presenting my ass good and high for him. His palm smacked my right butt-cheek with a crack like a starting pistol, and I felt his thick cock-head mash into the complex wetness of my sex. He pushed, trying to find an angle. But it took Freda's hands to guide him in, spreading my inner labia safely out of the target zone.

"Whoa," he said through gritted teeth; "you're tight, little bitch."

I groaned, half in pleasure, half in dismay.

"There," Freda chided, and reached underneath me. I felt her nails score my mons before her fingers settled on my clit. Oh, that felt good: that big cock inside my bitch cunt, and her expert caress on the button of my arousal. There was no more fear and no more discomfort, despite his considerable girth. Slowly at first, gaining confidence in my ability to take it, he powered into my slippery hole with thrust after thrust until his balls were slapping against my pussy. He filled me and reshaped me and gripped me tight, his fingers biting into my hips and ass, his thighs drumming against me. I could feel the whine of need inside me growing to a great howl.

Twisting, I rammed my head against Dev's pelvis, rubbing my face across his crotch. The thick rubber of his kilt stopped his erection from showing to the outside world, but I could feel the hard knot of his cock against my cheek. I licked at the rubber, tasting talc, panting.

"Please!" I squealed, forgetting my role. "Please!"

Suddenly galvanized, he tugged frantically at one buckled strap after another. Victor's cock was like a hammer pounding inside me. Dev made an opening big enough to pop his dick out into view, and I fell upon it with my mouth, sucking it deep into my throat. The more Victor thrust and Freda rubbed, the deeper

I could take Dev. I didn't need to breathe. I didn't need to think. I only had one goal—and in minutes I was there. I screamed around Dev's cock as my orgasm exploded.

That was enough for Dev. He let loose down my throat, pumping his cream into me, filling my mouth so that I choked and snorted and guzzled it all down, like the greedy little bitch I am. Victor rammed harder and harder into the burning glow of my meltdown.

"Stop now," said Freda, stepping back. "Pull out."

Without hesitation, Victor pushed away from me, leaving a gaping void in my life.

"Hands behind your head."

I swallowed the last of Dev's cum and looked behind me, shocked. Victor stood with arms up, staring into space, his face twisted with frustration, his skin gleaming with sweat. He must have been right on the brink; his cock was a great glistening spear thrust out before him. But he was a true sub: far more obedient than any dog would have been.

"That'll do. Follow me." Freda looked over at Dev. "I hope his service satisfied."

"Very much so. Thank you." Dev was short of breath but admirably collected as he tucked his cock out of sight.

Freda nodded graciously and then turned away, unsheathing her riding whip. Victor followed in her footsteps as she led him toward the playroom and the punishment that was his reward. There was a scattering of nervous applause as the circle of watchers made way. Many moved to follow. They wanted to see.

I let my legs collapse under me. "Poor dog," I whispered.

"She wants him to last out the night." Dev bent and embraced me, sliding one arm beneath my thighs, plucking me from the bench. I curled up against his chest, licked his ear, then kissed him. I knew he liked to taste his own cum on my lips.

"I love you, Master."

"Was it good, Princess?"

"Very good, Master. Very very good. Thank you."

"You were fucking incredible. Just beautiful." He kissed my hair and carried me across the room, to the comfortable seat and the water I suddenly desperately needed. Snuggling up in his lap, I felt Dev's hand slip between my thighs, exploring the gape of my used sex. As he pressed my clit I groaned, shifting against him.

"What?" he growled. "More?"

"What does it say on my tag, Master? You know me."

"I do. You're my naughty little bitch."

"Yes, Master." I brushed my lips against his. "All yours."

LAST CALL

Alison Tyler

I want the bartender to close and lock the front door of the bar. "What happens in The Local stays in The Local" I want some wiseass to say. There will be laughter, of the nervous variety, and the men will try not to look into each other's eyes. Because what we're going to do here is a gang bang, and brother, when you say those words aloud, people get jittery.

This isn't noncon, mind you. I am not asking for something from *Last Exit to Brooklyn*. Don't leave me unconscious on an old vinyl car seat behind the bar. Yes, I want the abuse, but I want to revel in every moment. In fact, I want to name the lineup. That's why we have to wait until closing time, when everyone else can leave except for the five men I've chosen.

Choosing was the difficult part. Which five? And even more curious—*why* five? Five is the number I've decided on tonight because I think that's what I can take. Five guys in a line. One after the other. Or five guys in a circle, coming on my naked skin.

I won't start out naked. I want to be clothed and mussed. I

want my opaque black tights pulled down, my panties tugged until the seams give way. This outfit was purposefully chosen for the thin material that will tear easily. I would have worn a dress made of paper if one were readily available.

Closing time's coming. I look at the clock over the bar. The boys are starting to shuffle around. I can tell that they want the rest of the crowd to leave as much as I do. *Stumble home, people. Get into your trucks, shut one eye, and hope you make the ride home alive. However you do it, get the fuck out.* My five are all hard. I can tell. They are about to come in their pants, and we haven't even started.

How did I choose the team?

Number one goes without saying. He's my man. Declan wants this to happen as much as I do. We talk about nothing else when we're in bed, his hand on my throat, his cock to the hilt inside me. "How many can you take?" he likes to ask. "Could you do three? Four? How many could you work, baby?"

Tonight, we're finally going to find out.

Next up? The bartender. He's young yet, and baby-faced. He thinks he's all that and a bag of chips. Why shouldn't he? The girlies in town take their turns riding his cock and his pretty blond mustache. But we're going to age him tonight.

The chef—if you can call him that, more of a fry cook—he's third. Why? Because the big guy seems lonely, and I've always been a compassionate sort. He's good-looking, with an extra solid forty pounds on his six-foot frame and a guilty look in his eyes all the time. What type of porn does he have stashed under his single twin? I'd like to know.

Fourth is a friend going through the type of divorce that makes men believe all women are cunts. Flynn is bitter and angry. I want him to take that aggression out on me. *Call me her name,* I plan on telling him. *Make it hurt.*

Five is a drifter. He's not a local. But he's the kind of guy who has always made me perk up and take notice. He's lean and hard-bodied in his old buffalo-plaid flannel shirt and worn Levi's. He looks as if he has done some serious fighting in his life—hands all scarred to shit—but he also has that glint in his eyes. Yeah, he's done some serious fucking, as well.

The other four know that this is a gang bang. The drifter? I simply asked if he'd stay on after closing. He gave me a look of mild interest, tracing me up and down with his dark blue eyes, and said he didn't have anywhere better to be.

How can we do a gang bang in a small town like ours? We're all friends here. Or if not friends, at least not enemies. We all know each other. That's my point. This could be a problem in some places. How can I sashay in next Friday night after having been spread out on the pool table tonight, whipped and fucked by neighbors?

Like I said, tonight we're finally going to find out.

Here's my thought on the matter: We all know each other's secrets here. Why not add one more? Look, I don't want to be one of those women who reaches the end of her road and thinks, *Why not? What the fuck was I waiting for?* I want to sit there on my front porch in my rocker and have shimmering nights like these to remember.

The regulars are starting to leave. Last call ends the show. My five are shifting. Yeah, they're hard. All of them. The chef keeps stepping forward and peering through the doorway from the kitchen. The bartender drops a glass, something I've never seen him do before. My man has his hand on my waist, his mouth on my neck. He's kissing me and telling me how fucking sexy I am and how proud of me he is. Our buddy, touching the spot where his ring used to be, looks as if he can't wait to come in my face and make me like it. And the drifter? He toys with his half-empty shot glass on the bar, clearly waiting to take his cues from the rest of us.

Say you want a guy to tie you up, and you might win a raised eyebrow. Ask for a spanking, and there's a pussy type of man who will raise his hand—not to smack your ass, but in protest—and tell you he doesn't go in for that sort of thing. But confess that what you really desire, what keeps you up in the night, is to have a line of men take turns fucking you, and you'll find out who your friends truly are.

The bar's quiet now. The door is locked, front light out. We're all sitting exactly where we were when Brody hollered "Last call." Then the cook comes out to lean against the bar. He grips a beer in one big mitt and stares at me. The bartender, always so damn cocky in the past, lifts a bottle of vodka from the shelf and pours himself a shot on the largish side. Declan starts to kiss me, his mouth hot on mine, his hands roaming over my body. I'm sitting next to his buddy, Flynn, and I feel Flynn move in tighter to me. We haven't talked rules—because how can you do that? How can you run down the rules to a gang bang if you've never participated in one before? I have the feeling that this is the sort of activity that grabs momentum as the event progresses. Because right now, there's just Declan kissing me and Flynn's hands on my body.

Oh, wait. *That's* new. Flynn is running his hands along my back while Declan kisses my neck. I have my eyes closed until the scrape of a chair catches my attention. Is it the cook coming closer? The drifter taking off? No, it's Brody, setting upside-down chairs onto the nearby tables, as if this were any other closing night on any other night of the week.

But it's not. Flynn lifts my hair and starts to kiss the nape of my neck. A shiver works through me. The cook walks closer to us. He says, "Did you mean what you said before?"

What'd I say before? You're wondering, aren't you? I'd leaned in while he was cooking, and I waited until he looked my way. Then I said, "Joe, you've always wanted to fuck me, haven't you?"

People don't get to talk like that very often. Do you know what I mean? Most of the day, we walk around stifling our inner selves, damping down on the words we'd love to let loose. But I thought, *Fuck that. Tonight, I'm going to get what I want or flame out trying.* Joe had looked at me and said, "Hell yeah, Dina. You break up with Dec yet?"

When I shook my head, his eyebrows shot up, and I simply said, "If you're game, stay on after closing." Declan had a similar convo with Brody. And now we're all here, and Flynn has moved me onto the closest table, and Declan is pushing my dress to my hips and Brody's coming forward, clearly unsure what to do, but not so unsure he won't make a move. He's young, but he's a bartender. He's had his share of girls.

"This an every Friday night occasion?" That's the drifter. He's smoking even though you're not allowed to smoke in a bar in California anymore. But we've got bigger secrets to keep than that.

"No," says Declan, "Not every Friday." And I giggle because I can't help myself. I'm spread on a table, soft woven dress to my hips, Joe stroking my hair off my face, Flynn surprisingly gentle with his mouth on my fingertips. And this drifter wants to know if we do this all the time.

Flynn takes my hand and places my palm against the bulge in his slacks. When was the last time I touched another man's cock? A man aside from my husband? More than ten years. I trace my fingers along the rise of his erection, and I sigh because this is happening. Finally and for real.

I cup his balls through his jeans, and Flynn presses forward to gain more contact. I wonder for a second if I'm going to be graceful enough to figure this out. I've never had much rhythm. But then Brody kisses me, moving aside Flynn and Declan. He leans down and kisses me, and I think that I don't have to worry so much after all. The guys will do all the shifting and choreographing for me. I let myself go in the kiss. I kiss him the way I have always wanted to, every time I walk into the bar. Because girls want things, too. Guys don't hold the patent on lusting after what you're not supposed to have. I sigh as he pulls away, and I close my eyes.

When you're single, you can walk into a bar and pick your man. You can make eyes at the bartender. You can flirt with the chef. You can focus on a drifter and decide that yeah, maybe tonight you'll sample a bit of strange. There's excitement on every horizon. How will that bartender fuck you? Bent over a bar stool? In his pickup truck? Out in the woods, where nobody can hear? What does the fry cook like to watch when nobody's home? Man-on-man porn, right? He'll let you lick his asshole and fuck him with a strap-on, so long as you don't tell anyone later. And the drifter? Oh, I miss my one-night stands with the men passing through. Men whose names I'd forget later, but I'd remember the connection. And maybe a flicker or two of something else. Like finding a hidden scar way up high under a shirt sleeve. Or seeing a girl's name tattooed somewhere sacred.

But when you're part of the old-and-married club, the tools get rusty. You're not supposed to want to fuck anyone else, anymore, ever again. Take your libido, honey. Bottle it up in that mason jar and stick the thing on a shelf. No more surprises for you, dearie. You're all used up.

Things start to move faster now. I think Declan has been waiting for someone to show a sign of life, and that someone is

Brody. Brody, whose kiss I still feel on my lips, the taste of his vodka on my tongue.

I sense the men moving around me. Declan tells me to open my mouth, and I do, not surprised at all to find a naked cock at my lips. I keep my eyes closed still, as if I have a blindfold on, because it's still easier that way. I know right away that it's Declan's cock I'm sucking. After more than a decade together, I am well versed in the girth and the ridges that make this cock feel like home to me. I suck him on my back. He lets me work at my own pace. Then I moan—I can't help myself—because there's a mouth between my legs, on my pussy through my panties and my hose.

Who is that? I would like to know, would like to peek, but in this position, even if I opened my eyes, I'd only have a view of cock and balls.

"Put out your hands," Declan says, and I realize I have my fists clenched tight at my sides. I spread my arms open, palms open, and in seconds I have a dick in each hand. Am I stroking off Flynn? Jerking off the stranger? I don't look. I don't ask. My tights are getting wet in the center. The man between my legs is sucking at the nylon.

I sense the hesitation and then Declan says, "Take them off her."

My heels are pulled off, and then the hose. I shiver at the feeling of another man taking off my clothes. It hasn't happened in so fucking long. Then I feel a mustache against my thigh, and I know that's Brody between my legs. How funny that I've always yearned for a mustache ride, and now I'm getting my wish. His whiskers are sweet against my naked skin, his mouth warm and open over my panties. Declan moves and I open my eyes and blink. I am looking up into the eyes of Joe the chef and the nameless drifter. Joe's got a cock like I thought he would have.

Thick and long and hard. It suits him. The drifter's is thinner, but rigid. I was wrong. Flynn isn't close by. He's standing back, watching. His eyes are wet.

"Get her naked," Declan says.

Brody pulls my panties down then, and I raise my hips to help him, but I don't stop stroking those cocks. I feel energized, as if I could do this all night. The low, hungry sighs of the men is payment enough. I am the center, the focus of attention, and I bask in the glow.

Brody dives back between my thighs, and I bend my knees and splay for him, back arching. He's so good. Declan knows how to eat me, knows all the tricks and turns I love best. But there's something unreal about having that magic mustache run over my pussy lips and against my inner thighs.

Then suddenly, Flynn is in motion. "If we're going to do this, we should really do this," he says, surprising me. He's not my husband. But he takes charge, nonetheless, gripping me in his arms and carrying me to a low, heavy wooden table in the back of the room. He pulls my dress off me, leaving me totally naked. Then he motions to Brody, who gets on the table first as if he and Flynn have had a private conversation, and then he positions me over Brody's mouth, on my hands and knees.

"Like that," he says as Brody resumes licking my pussy. "You," he points to Joe. "You start."

"Start?" Joe's cock is in his hand. He's jerking it as he talks.

"Let her suck you."

Joe looks to Declan, who nods, and then he steps forward. I part my lips and take him in. He's so nice and thick. I suck him as sweetly as I can, thinking of how lonely he seems, how needy. I make the most of the seconds he's in my mouth before Flynn grabs his shoulders and says, "Now fuck her."

For a second, everything stops, even Brody's tongue on my

clit. There's an edge to Flynn's tone. But maybe we needed this. Someone to take command. Joe moves behind me and begins to slip his cock into my pussy. I'm swollen and wet. So wet. Brody continues to lick my clit as Joe fucks me. I turn my head and see that Declan is pressed back against the wall, watching everything.

Flynn grabs onto the drifter. "Now, you," he says. "What's your name?"

"Matthew."

"Matt, let her suck you."

The drifter gets in front of me, and I open my mouth for him. He looks over his shoulder, and I know he's getting approval from Declan. That he knows who the boss really is. His cock tastes like ocean water. I suck him to the rhythm that Joe is fucking me, to the beat that Brody is licking me and I groan at the sensation of being so well cared for.

Joe starts to speed up, and I realize he's going to come. He grips my hips and pounds into me, then pulls out at the last moment and shoots all over my back. I shiver at the sensation. I'm wearing another man's come. I wonder if someone will grab the bar towel, wipe me clean.

But Flynn is like a machine. He pulls Joe away, puts the drifter into place and then turns to look at Declan. "You up, man?"

Dec grins at him. "Flynn," he says in a kind voice, "I'm last."

The drifter is in my pussy, and his cock seems to reach further than Joe's did. I see Joe moving to pour himself a drink behind the bar. Flynn takes his spot in front of me. Brody is busy licking my clit like a good boy. Flynn strokes my hair and looks into my eyes. I was there on his wedding day. I was at his house when he found out his wife was cheating. I see all the pain in his eyes, and I see that he wants to imbue some of that onto me. And I want to take it.

The drifter drags his fingernails down my sides, and I shiver. He palms the cheeks of my ass, spreads them a bit to see my hole. I see him in the mirror as he motions to Joe, who is watching with a glass in hand.

"Come here," he says, and Joe walks closer. I watch in the mirror as Joe and Matthew kiss while Matthew's fucking me. He pulls out before coming, and the two start to make out against the wall, Matthew's dick shiny with my juices, Joe's big fist working around the shaft.

Flynn, who was gentle at the start, who was unsure for the first few minutes, begins to face-fuck me, and I never miss a beat. I suck him like a pro, and I'm pleased with myself. I drain him before he can stop himself from coming. I'm every woman he's ever loved, and every bitch he's ever hated, and he howls as he comes down my throat. There's no undoing that. Whenever he sees me from now on, he will own this moment. He backs off me, and he's no longer in charge.

Now there's Brody on the table and Declan stepping forward.

"Suck him," Dec says. "Suck his cock."

I undo Brody's jeans and set him free.

"Suck him while I fuck you," Dec instructs, and I do what he says, licking the precome from the head of Brody's cock and then sucking him while Declan takes his proper place behind me. Brody has to lean upward to keep contact with my clit, and I'm on my elbows with my ass in the air.

"You're so pretty," Declan says, and it's like there's only him and me in the room, except for the cock between my lips and the tongue on my clit. Except for the fact that Joe and Matthew are fucking against the bar and Flynn is lighting up one of Matthew's cigarettes.

Declan slaps my ass and grabs my hair. He fucks me hard, and I come, Brody licking my clit like a beast and then shooting into my mouth. I would collapse against the bartender, but Declan lifts me up, carries me to the hallway and presses me up against the wall. Now it is him and me, and he fucks me so hard, I feel like I've never been done before. Like this is the first time.

Which in a way it is.

The first gang bang. The first time I ever showed off who I really am deep inside. Dec comes in me and then spins me around and lifts me into his arms.

"The first of many," Dec promises with a smile.

HIGHLY INSPIRED

Alyssa Turner

"Welcome back Ms. Pierce. Glad you're joining us today."

I responded to her perky greeting with a polite smile. "Hi, Mandy. Full house, huh? Bet you're ready for the weekend. I know I am." Too bad it's only Thursday.

I'd flown that New York to DC air shuttle so many times before, I could use my frequent-flyer miles to get to the moon. The flight attendants treated me practically like family. Once again, buttoned up in my most conservative of business suits, I was the perfect image of corporate sterility, predictability, reliability. Ugh, what had happened to me? My life seemed like an endless blur of meetings and sales reports. Work had become who I was, not what I did, and I almost didn't recognize the person in the mirror anymore. That girl, the one who even surprised herself half the time—I wanted her back.

There was movement in the next seat and I glanced sideways at the reckless-looking guy in a tight-fitting skater tee and a sexy buzz cut raising the sun shield on the window. The warm rays hit my face and washed his dirty blond stubble in an amber glow. What a contrast between the two of us, though he looked to be about my same age. He removed his sunglasses from his collar and placed them on the tray table along with his cell phone, then flashed a smile when he caught me stealing a glimpse of his bad boy looks. I smiled back, but immediately returned to my papers.

"May I have your attention, please?" Mandy's tone hinted we weren't going to like what she had to say. "Dulles is experiencing some difficulties with several of their runways due to bad weather in the DC metro area. We expect about an hour delay on departure."

Above the loud hiss of the ventilation system, a united sigh of disappointment flooded the cabin and I called the office to let them know I'd be pressed to make the morning staff meeting on time. It seemed everyone was making calls, including my temporary neighbor.

When I was finished, I couldn't help but overhear, though he was careful to speak softly. "...Keep still. I'll have a taste of you soon, but not yet. I just want to look at you first."

I pulled my papers up to my face and smiled privately to myself, assuming he was talking to his girlfriend. The call went on for five minutes or so, making me blush at his words. Lucky girl, I mused. But it was odd that he didn't seem to say good-bye or end the conversation in any recognizable way. He simply finished with, "... and every last drop of you is delicious." Then, he ended the call.

I looked away—stared intentionally across the aisle to hide the guilt displayed on my face for eavesdropping. The moisture in my panties was thankfully not as obvious.

"Don't worry," he whispered, leaning just slightly closer with a playful smirk. "I'm not a serial obscene phone caller." When I turned to him with a frown, he smiled. "Well, not exactly."

My expression turned quizzical.

"I'm Russell. Sorry if you were offended by that. I was trying to speak softly, but..." he trailed off with a more tempered look on his face. "You flying on business?"

"Yes," I responded tightly, picking up reading where I had left off on my reports. He was cute as hell, but that didn't mean he wasn't a nut job.

Russell sighed. "Really, I don't bite; what you heard—that was just work. Lots of women are willing to pay good money for a little phone sex to brighten their day." He looked bashful about it all of a sudden, glancing at the phone sitting on the tray table in front of him. "Twenty bucks a pop. Paid for grad school doing it."

"Sounds wild," I said, with a tentative glance.

He sucked his teeth. "Yeah, well, it was big fun when I first started—beat the hell out of waiting tables, I'll tell you that. But after five years, I'm just tired of it."

"Really?" I was fascinated.

"You do something for long enough it eventually becomes like any other job—same ole shit, ya know? I make like fifteen, twenty calls a day sometimes to my regulars."

"Ever catch them at a bad time? I mean...you know, it's not always convenient to talk like that."

He laughed. "I do all the talking. 'Bout the only thing I ever hear them say is 'excuse me, I've got to take this.'"

"Why don't they call you? Is it always a surprise?" My mouth was open with a wondrous grin, my head shaking slowly as I absorbed what he told me. Never had I heard of such a thing.

"They know approximately when I'll call, but not exactly. It's more impulsive that way—makes them feel chased after... desired, I guess."

"Hmm," I said with an ironic chuckle.

"What's funny?"

"I was just sitting here thinking about how my corporate career was suffocating the life out of me, and secretly envying you."

"Envying me?" He cocked his head to the side with real interest.

"You seemed like such a rebel. Now I know you're just a slave to the system like I am."

He laughed with me. "A corporate slave and a phone whore, what a pair."

"I'm Chloe."

"Great to meet you, Chloe." His smile was genuine, as sexy as his softly creased eyes and broad cheekbones.

"Do you ever meet these women in person?" It would've been a shame if they had no idea how ridiculously hot he was.

"No, just phone sex. Never the real deal with my clients." He laughed again. "Anyway, I get way more action on the phone than I can handle, believe me." He scratched his chin and gazed at me for a moment before exploring the reading material stashed in the seat pocket in front of him.

I could say that I didn't know what possessed me. It would be easy to claim temporary insanity or a bipolar episode, PMS or an out-of body-experience. Anything would be easier than just admitting the truth. I simply wanted to do something outrageous for a change. I felt a surge of adrenaline sting me and I looked around, noting the passengers across the aisle were busy with their own magazines or dozing off.

Impulsively, I eased closer to him with a secretive whisper, "How about some fresh inspiration?" Logic wasn't in control. Ambition didn't have a say in my actions. It wasn't a career move—just a downright crazy idea, but simply irresistible given the circumstances of my present state of mind and his.

He looked confused and I placed my hand under the tray table and onto his thigh to clarify my meaning.

"Why don't you make another one of your calls?"

A quick flick of his finger and he pressed send, searching my face for a clue of what was to come of this. My hand crept farther under the tray and into his crotch. Soon enough his trepidation gave way to eager compliance as his words started to flow like heavy molasses: "You come home to find me in your bed. I've been stroking myself for half an hour already, waiting for you."

I sent my fingertips in search of the outline of his cock, tracing the edges through his jeans.

"I'm as hard as a rock, just thinking about those beautiful legs wrapped around my waist."

I relished the way his cock was indeed growing hard, pressing against the denim and thrilling me with the whole concept of getting him hot while he went to work on his client.

He continued, "You look so damn sexy standing there watching me. I can't wait to have you." Surely she was on the other end envisioning his words. While he spoke, he looked directly into my eyes, hardly blinking and taking slow deep breaths between sentences. "Let's see if you're as anxious as I am."

He unzipped his jeans, allowing me stealthy access to his thickening shaft beneath the cover of the small plastic table. Through that amazingly convenient opening in his briefs, I took him, warm and firm in my concealed grip, under the tray. Placing the phone to my ear, he gave me a chance to hear her moan softly. No doubt she was acting on her own impulses somewhere in the world and ready to see how far Russell would take her today. I pictured her rubbing her clit in her office, perhaps, with the door closed; her mind placing him between her legs. The vision rushed through me with a blast of heat to my core.

"Pull down your panties and turn around. You made me wait long enough," he growled.

Every word on his lips had me aching a little more inside. Every stroke of my hand enticed a more ragged breath from his chest. I'd started to squirm in my seat when Mandy appeared at my side, standing in the aisle. My busy hand froze inside Russell's pants and he turned toward the window, muffling his conversation behind his palm.

"Can I get you anything? You're coffee with two creams, right?" Mandy asked. But when her eyes found the trail of my arm leading to Russell's lap and her gaze traveled back to my blushing face, she had another idea. "How about a blanket," she offered with a wink and reached to open the stowage hatch above our seats. "It's chilly in here—might want to cover up."

"Thanks," I breathed, and she continued down the aisle and flashed me a firecracker grin over her shoulder.

Russell gave me an inquisitive look, and I shook my head in reassurance that everything was cool.

The blanket was a score, allowing me to flick his button loose and pull his cock out of his pants entirely. I only wished I could see it. The smooth skin slid easily in my hand over a thick head that wanted for my attention. Licking my lips, I imagined them wrapped onto it and suddenly remembered how much I liked having a cock in my mouth.

His voice was full of hushed gravel for this woman, words camouflaged by the whooshing of air pouring from the overhead vents. "You like it when I stick my finger in your ass, don't you? Fuck that sweet pussy and stroke that tight little asshole of yours, is that what you want?"

He shared the phone with me again and I heard her say that

she was going to come, the unmistakable hum of her favorite toy in the background.

I increased my pace on his cock, pretending to be interested in watching the baggage trucks on the tarmac through his window. His lips quivered and his words were shaky, and I couldn't stop smiling over the entire scene—so very, very unprofessional. And then it was over, the call ending much like the other, with her satisfaction no doubt laced between the words on his tongue and her proficient self-service. He placed his hand on top of mine and put down the phone.

Russell looked me over, swallowing hard and steadying his breathing. I followed as his tongue made a brief appearance against his bright teeth. He held absolutely still and he leaned into my ear.

"Your turn to get some work done now, beautiful." He blew the words into my hair and sent a shiver over my skin.

Giddy over the prospect, I gathered my papers into a neat pile on my tray and picked up a pen, while Russell made sure the blanket was suitably arranged.

From that moment on, a sales report would never make me sigh with boredom again. He snuck a hand below the blanket and encouraged my legs apart. My gray rayon skirt retreated to my thighs and a simple adjustment in my chair allowed it to curl practically around my waist. Satisfied, Russell tapped on the papers, prodding me to get to work.

Units per quarter up thirty percent. I made my first notation on the chart. Though my writing meandered into illegibility when Russell guided his fingers under the lacy waistband of my panties.

"Your boss will be upset with you if you show up unprepared," he chided, finding the swell of my clit between two digits and tugging upward on it gently.

I pressed my lips together and tried to keep writing, challenging myself to concentrate.

"You're a good little worker bee for the hive aren't you?" he breathed, tickling my earlobe with his tongue. I nodded, and let a tiny whimper escape my lips. Russell curled one of those fingers and without hesitation, slid into me. My back straightened as I bit back a moan.

"The captain has turned on the FASTEN YOUR SEATBELTS sign. Please turn off all electronic devices and place your trays and seat backs in the upright position as we prepare for take off." Mandy and the others started their check of the cabin and I was obliged to sacrifice the cover our tray tables afforded us. Just the blanket and my stack of papers now disguised the curious position of his hand.

"This is going to be a long slow ride, Chloe. You think you can handle it?" Russell asked, holding his place in my panties while his finger moved like time standing painfully still.

Handle an hour and a half of wishing he could bend me over in this aisle? I wasn't sure. "Guess we're about to find out," I replied, finding his cock under the blanket bobbing freely against my hand. "I can see you're enjoying yourself."

He smiled and nodded, settling back into his seat with eyes closed. Then he nodded again when he sent his finger slowly into the slick river pooling around it.

I was high on his touch, the slow churn of lust swallowing me whole. Russell worked his middle finger in a circle and wound me up until I was ready to pop—never had I been so wet, so drowned in need. Many thoughts passed through my hazy mind, like how gloriously insane it was to have a perfect stranger soaking his fingers with my juices, and the desperate hope that he wouldn't stop. But mostly, I thought about landing and rushing that man to the nearest restroom.

Russell kept me dangling on the edge of an orgasm the entire flight, slowing his slippery maneuvers to a stop when I started to shake, and creeping back into motion once I'd steadied under his hand.

"This is the most fun I've had in a long time, Chloe," he said to me on my third threat to overflow.

"Me too," I purred, "but if you think this is fun..."

"We'll be landing soon. I have a connecting flight to Miami I'm supposed to catch in twenty minutes."

"I'm expected at a conference table in an hour."

The plane bucked as it met with the ground.

"You could call out sick," he said with a raised eyebrow.

"And you could catch another flight. What's in Miami anyway?"

"A three o'clock interview for a real job in civil engineering."

"Go figure."

"I wish I could have you, even for a few minutes," he whispered directly in my ear.

"A few minutes wouldn't do us justice, we both know that."

There was a long pause while I weighed my options and he seemed to be doing the same. As the plane came to a halt and the FASTEN YOUR SEATBELTS signs went dark, both of us picked up our cell phones.

The hotel next to the airport would do just fine, since close was the only credential that interested us. We strode through the sliding glass doors with our carry-ons, looking like the quintessential odd couple—grit and grace. I'd feigned a stomach virus and Russell rescheduled for the following afternoon. The next twenty-four hours we would be off the grid, working on our impulses and nothing else.

With condoms purchased at the lobby convenience shop in

hand, he'd hardly swiped the key card before I blurted, "Can you believe we're doing this?"

"Not really."

In the room, with the noonday sun breaking past the tacky green drapes, neither of us knew what to do first, to taste first. He reached for the buttons on my blouse, rubbing the highest one between his thumb and his finger. I started with the buttons at the bottom and met him halfway. His mouth lingered over my moistened lips, his tongue calling for a playmate with teasing licks. One hand released my blouse and it fell from my shoulders to the floor. The other cupped the back of my head as he worked his tongue into a frenzy. I tore at his T-shirt, dying to feel his skin against mine in the cool recycled air.

Russell broke free from my lips to rid himself of his clothes, shedding his shirt and hastily peeling his fitted jeans from his lean thighs. His cock sprung forward, looking as delicious as I had imagined and I wanted nothing more but to suck the hell out of it. With bunched denim still constraining his calves, I took him to the back of my throat causing him to waver off balance. He curled his fingers into my hair and tangled them among my straightened tresses tightly enough to make me gasp. I filled my mouth with him, bumping my tonsils with his cock and tasting his precome every time. I didn't know his last name, but I thought it should be Stover, for how sweet he tasted.

"Damn, that feels good."

Just because I was a little out of practice was no reason to start slacking. In that polyester-laden hotel room, I was on vacation from the life that awaited me in my briefcase. My hair a toussled mess around a greedy mouth, Russell seemed to like my wild alter ego, growling his appreciation. I liked the way he was looking at me.

"So good, Chloe."

He pulled my head forward with each stroke, and I was beginning to ache beyond patience for a fucking of another kind. My wandering fingers didn't go unnoticed.

"You want some of this, don't you?"

I answered by retreating to the bed, fussing with the zipper on my skirt.

"No, leave it on," he grinned, as he stepped out of his shoes and pants. "Come over here, to the chair."

Topless, I met him at the plush armchair by the window. He parted the drapes, revealing the bustling street below full of midday travelers mostly in business attire. As he rushed my skirt up over my ass and pulled the soaking strip of black lace askew, I climbed onto the seat cushion, holding steady to the chair back. I don't think I've been as pleased by anything in a long time.

It wasn't the way he grabbed my hips or how easily he slipped inside, though both sensations made me coo like a baby. I'd spotted a woman in basic gray wool trousers and a black overcoat, toting her laptop and quick stepping it to the terminal with her nose in her BlackBerry. The glee of being here instead of there turned my coos into howls of triumph. Russell rode my screams to their highest pitch, making me grip the worn velvet cushion with white knuckles and then claw at the drapes as he pressed me harder, encouraging me against the cool glass with my breasts on full display for anyone who chanced a glance at our second-story window.

Standing now in the seat with me in relentless pursuit, he grabbed one of my thighs and leveraged it high against his upward thrusts, nudging at my orgasm with his deep strokes. I called his name out, because truly it was the only thing I could think of in the delirium of my sensory overload. Nothing else mattered, no reports, no meetings—just the tingles of delight that beautiful man without a last name was gunning into my cunt. Sounds of my satisfaction dropped off my lips in short bursting sighs until he bottomed out inside me.

"Can I call you?"

I sauntered over to him nude, with his scent awash on me, and tucked my card into his front pocket. "I hope you do."

He clutched my wrist and brought my fingers to his mouth for one last taste of our sex. "On the house, of course."

I laughed, rolling my eyes with playful exaggeration, "That's generous of you, Russell."

He stood in the doorway, hesitating.

"You're going to miss your flight," I uttered with regret for the words.

He tapped on the doorframe a few times and inhaled deeply in a knowing sigh.

Rising on tiptoe, I stretched to reach his lips and he met them with sweet intensity, dizzying me again, instantly.

"Good-bye, Chloe."

"'Bye, Russell."

As I closed the door behind him, my phone vibrated on the night table across the room.

"Oh yes, I feel much better now... Four o'clock meeting? I'll be there."

AIR CONDITIONING. COLOR TV.
LIVE MERMAIDS.

Anna Meadows

He first saw her through the glass, turning in the water so her hair whipped behind her. She'd grown it out. It billowed and rippled to her waist. It must have taken her an hour a night to comb it. She never used to let it grow past her shoulders, or the Santa Anas would tangle it so bad she couldn't even get it into two braids. He'd never told her how much he liked it that way, all wild and weedy from crawling through the grass to catch ladybugs or spinning on the tire swing. He'd watched her from the tree house then, her hair fanning out like black sea oats.

He knew the shape of her body, not so different from the summer they graduated high school. She had that same softness in her thighs—he could see that even through the mermaid tail, covered in sequins the color of a peacock. But if he didn't know her by her body, he would have known her by how her hair spread out in the water, the same way it did in the pond back home, like she was falling.

"House beer's half off," the bartender said. "Looks like you need it."

Daniel ordered one but didn't drink it. He was still watching her.

He'd been on his way home to visit family for the holiday weekend when he saw the sign on the side of the highway. MERMAID MOTEL. HOME OF DIVE IN THE DESERT. AIR-CONDITIONING. COLOR TV. LIVE MERMAIDS. He turned off and got a room—he was tired enough that if he stopped, it'd have to be for the night—because the last two words on the sign made him think of Lila, turning underwater in the pond.

"One day I'm gonna be a mermaid," she'd said every time she came up for air. She always had on a one-piece, because her mother never let her wear anything else. "Only *putas* wear those two-pieces," Mrs. Ramirez would call out the window as they got on their bikes. It just made Daniel want Lila more, thinking of her belly staying pale as her shoulders browned. Her costume at Dive in the Desert may have been her first two-piece, a bra so heavy with teal rhinestones it flattened her breasts, and a mermaid tail with a fin so big that carrying it around must've tired her out by the end of her shift.

Dive in the Desert was the bar in the downstairs of the Mermaid Motel, fifty-nine dollars a night, and that was in the high season. The filled seats in the bar usually numbered more than twice the daily check-ins at the Mermaid. The bar was on the trucking highway, the Ocean Floor Onion Rings were supposed to be the best in the state, and when a mermaid came out, the house beer was half off. The owner once had big plans, a nightly show with a half-dozen mermaids all flicking their tails at the long-haul truckers. But after he got the kitchen up to code, he only had enough money left for a secondhand aquarium, just big enough for one mermaid, two if one of them was Lila. She was so short that she fit in the tank with one of the other girls. That was why the owner had hired her, even though she had little boobs and her hair hadn't quite been long enough at the time.

"It'll grow," Lila had said, standing in his office in her jean shorts and a ten-year-old T-shirt from the Grand Canyon. "My hair, I mean."

Lila was still learning, but now she knew how to flip in the tank, twisting her hips like the older mermaids taught her. "It makes all the little jewels get the light," Yolanda had said. Lila was usually with one of them—she was good at getting out of the way, even with that big tail—but today she was on her own. The other mermaids had family to see for the holiday weekend, and while most places got booked up, nobody was making the drive to the middle of the Mojave to check in to the Mermaid Motel. Even the long-haul truckers went home if they could get the time off. The bar would be almost empty if it weren't for families making pit stops on road trips to somewhere else. The bar was getting more orders for grilled cheese sandwiches than gin and tonics. The little girls came up to the tank and pointed, and the boys tapped on the glass like Lila was a fish. She waved as she swam past, blowing a kiss with a string of little air bubbles.

Through the glass, she saw a man standing by himself at the other side of the bar, as far as he could get from the tank and still watch her. He had hair the color of the *masa de harina* Lila and her mother used to mix with water to make corn tortillas. He was about the right age, twenty-five or so, same as her, but she knew it wasn't Daniel. She'd thought she'd seen him at least ten times since she started at Dive in the Desert. Every time a young-looking guy with hair the color of sand-soil showed up in jeans, she'd see the blur of him through the water and the glass, and she'd think it was him. But every time she surfaced enough to peek over the edge of the tank, she was wrong. By now she'd given up looking and didn't come up until she needed the air so much her lungs grew tight in her rib cage.

The ketchup-and-french-fry crowd thinned out. Her shift ended. She rinsed off at the showerhead behind the bar, shielded by stacks of old crates. She left the costume on to rinse it out, the fin folded under her feet. Her eyes stung with the salt, and the turquoise sky blurred into the terra-cotta of the desert.

She shut off the water. Her vision was still a little fuzzy, but not enough that she didn't notice the man standing just on the other side of the crates. She startled. It wasn't the first time a drunk man had tried to watch one of the mermaids rinse the smell of the tank out of her hair, but they were usually looking for Sarah Jane, with that hair so blonde it looked white in the light of the tank, or Yolanda, with her breasts that spilled into her sequined bra like batter into a muffin tin.

Lila held her hands over her costume top. "Get out of here."

"All right," the man said. "But I'm waiting you out. I'll be in the lobby."

She recognized the voice, a little lower than she remembered, but with the same slow, even rhythm.

She rubbed her eyes to get the last of the salt out. "Daniel?"

The shape of him came into focus, a Polaroid developing. He had his hands in the pockets of his jeans, like always. Without pockets, he never knew what to do with them.

She laughed, and he slipped in between the stacks of crates and put his arms around her, like he would with a friend he hadn't seen in a while. But it didn't feel right. He and Lila had never been that way.

"What are you doing here?" she asked.

"Just stopped for the night," he said.

"Nobody stops here unless they get a flat or an overheated radiator."

She smelled like rock salt and desert and sky, a scent that was waiting on her skin when they were growing up, but now was as strong as open lilies.

She held her hand to the front of his shirt, damp now, and sticking to him. "I'm getting you wet," she said, and laughed again.

"I don't care." He held her again, but this time her mouth ended up on the patch of his shirt just over his collarbone. Her wet fingers pulled down the collar of his shirt, and she put her lips to the base of his neck.

She took in the scent of him. He still smelled like wet grass, like he slept in it every night. She stood on her toes to move her lips up his neck, the balls of her feet gripping the ground through the fabric of her tail. She tasted the light dusting of salt that perspiration had left on his skin. His hands gripped her waist, and he stopped holding her like a sister or an old friend.

He picked her up like she was something strange and pretty he'd found on a beach hundreds of miles from the desert. She put her arms around him, feeling the warmth of his back through his shirt, and kissed the rest of the salt off his neck. Her tail dripped on the asphalt and then the dry dirt parking lot. When the sun hit those tacky little rhinestones, they shimmered on her body like malachite. The men getting some air outside the bar were too drunk to notice, the women at the motel check-in desk too bored. A girl on the way to the car with her family pointed and said she saw the mermaid, but her mother didn't look, and said no, the mermaids were inside in the water where they could breathe.

The door to Daniel's room fell shut behind them, and he laid her down on the bed. Her hair and her tail soaked the sheets, and the whole room smelled like salt water. He helped her wriggle out of her tail and freed her breasts from her costume top. She'd wanted to be a mermaid worse than anything else since she was five years old, but right now shedding the weight of all those sequins made her feel like he'd woken her body up from a spell made of blue light and a shimmer of green. Like having his hands on her damp skin had turned her naked and human so she could part her legs.

She pulled his jeans down only as far as she needed to, and she slid under him. He hesitated, sure she couldn't mean for him to do that. He'd brought her back to his room to see her and touch her, to check her face and body against his memory and make sure he had it all right. But she put her hand on his back to tell him that, yes, this was what she wanted.

The soft ache of opening for him had the feel and color of something she wanted to taste, so much so that she almost made him pull out of her so she could put her mouth around his erection. She didn't. Instead she dug her heels into his lower back. He was gentle and slow, like she always guessed he would be. She loved that about him, like she loved how his hands were always in his pockets and how his hair was always just long enough to get in his eyes. But it made her so impatient she wrapped her legs around him tighter, lifting her butt and the small of her back up off the bed and closer to him so he was all the way inside her before he meant to be.

He caught a gasp in the back of his throat. She kissed him, and he eased her lips apart with his tongue. He was still inside her, but they laughed softly, just breathing, no real sound, because it was the first time they'd kissed since he'd shown up. It was the only part of it all that they'd done before, and they both wondered how they could've gotten so far without their lips touching.

She tightened around him, and they couldn't laugh anymore. The muscles inside her tensed and released, a rhythm she couldn't help, and he couldn't help finishing. His hand was already between her legs by the time he did. He traced his fingers around the little slick-wet pearl that made her thighs tremble the more he touched it. He couldn't remember when he started thinking of it that way, as her pearl. It was years before he ever touched it, years after the first time she said she wanted to be a mermaid, maybe sometime the summer after high school when she lived in that black one-piece. It had been strapless, her mother's one concession about swimsuits, so he'd been able to watch Lila's shoulders darken over those months.

Lila curled onto her side, pleasure blooming between her legs. At first she tried not to scream, then she remembered that nobody was out at the Mermaid Motel on a holiday weekend. The rooms on either side of Daniel's were probably empty. She let herself, and she could feel the shiver that her cry sent through him.

He held her as her breathing evened. She wondered if she should say thank you when a man made her feel like that, the same as if he held a door open or remembered what kind of *chiles* she liked.

Daniel kissed her back and caught the faint scent of the water in the tank. "Salt," he said. "Not chlorine?"

"Salt's cheaper," she said.

The hum of the air conditioner mixed with the sound of the ice machine turning over. It was a little like the buzz of the generator boxes and telephone lines in the neighborhood where they'd grown up.

"How'd you find me?" she asked.

"You were always saying you wanted to be a mermaid," he said. "How come you didn't tell me where you were going? One day I called and your mom just said you'd moved out."

The ice machine died down, but the air conditioner still called up the memory of lawn sprinklers. They'd talked about going to a hotel together, one day when they were older, but they'd meant one in the city, one nice enough that they didn't put VACANCY and PAY-PER-VIEW on their signs. But lying with him like this was putting Lila a little more on the side of cheap places with neon sides and bars next door.

"Why've you been hiding?" he asked.

"You were in college," she said. "Was I supposed to think you'd come back?"

"Yes," he said. He never had asked her why she didn't try going too. He'd always had two guesses and didn't like either one. Maybe she didn't have the money and didn't apply for scholarships. "We don't take charity from *los gringos*," her mother always told her. Or maybe it was because Mrs. Ramirez was always saying that girls shouldn't get too smart. But by then it was already too late for that. Lila was always smarter than Daniel and everybody else. She'd figured out how to lock her bedroom door with a skein of yarn and a few hairpins. She'd sewn old textbooks back together when the ones the school handed out were so worn the pages were falling out. That was how he knew, when she said she'd be a mermaid one day, that she'd do it.

"How long are you here for?" she asked.

He interlaced his fingers with hers and kissed the back of her hand. "I don't know," he said. "You tell me."

She reached behind her, her fingers tracing a path from his chest down to his crotch. He responded before she even touched him. She laughed in that way that scared him but always got him a little harder. Her costume, spread out on the floor like a skin she'd molted out of, caught the last of the afternoon sun through the blinds and cast comet trails of blue-green light on her body, still pale from the water. A girl turning under the surface of a pond, a woman in the coarse sheets and ice-machine white noise of a desert motel.

NIGHT SCHOOL

Valerie Alexander

Working the night shift at a small-town hotel is the ideal job for introverts. At city hotels, there are valets, bellhops and room service attendants in the lobby at any hour of the night. But at the Midwestern off-highway chain hotel where I worked as the night auditor, the silence was broken only by the sound of distant ice machines and the hum of the computer printing out the guest folios.

And the comings and goings of the escorts, of course.

I was three hours into my shift when the glass doors opened and the youngest of the usual male escorts came in. "Hey, Nina," Dalton said. As always, his smile at seeing me behind the desk seemed genuine. Not that it meant anything. He didn't see me that way. Most men didn't.

I waved casually, as if I hadn't been hoping that he would have a date in the hotel tonight. "Hi."

He sauntered to the elevator, pressed the button and leaned against the wall at the perfect angle to show off his long,

snake-hipped body. It had to be a gift, knowing how to show-
case himself like that. As usual, he was dressed in black with
his dark-blond hair artfully rumpled. Dalton tended to show
up for most of his dates looking like a knockoff James Dean,
though I'd seen him wear everything from polo shirts to basket-
ball jerseys to suits before. I assumed those were client requests.

The elevator pinged and the doors opened. He flashed me a
heart-melting smile and got on. As soon as the doors closed, I
checked my reflection. My red ponytail was in a state of collapse
and the shadows of insomnia circled my eyes. Oh, well. He
didn't notice my looks anyhow.

I'd never seen myself falling for a male escort. I'd never seen
myself falling for a pretty boy at all, let alone a twenty-year-old
who seduced men and women for a living. I'd been scoffing at
handsome men for as long as they'd been ignoring me. All cats
are gray in the dark, I would say to my friends. And I wanted
to believe that. But here I was, swooning over a professionally
devastating smile. It was mortifying.

I wondered who Dalton was seeing tonight and what they
would do. I knew most of his clients were men, though he saw
couples and the occasional woman, too. He was open with me
about what he did—once he'd figured out that I didn't care
about his doing business in the hotel, we'd fallen into the habit
of chatting after his dates. But he never shared too many details.
I wished he would. I wanted to picture it; wanted to know how
he took off his clothes, if he did it slowly with a boyish smile,
or if his clients preferred to unwrap him like a gift. I wanted to
know his techniques for pleasing clients; if he was better at being
forcefully passionate or tender and sensitive. I wanted to know
if he preferred men or women.

I wanted to know what it would be like if I hired him. If he
would stammer and get uncomfortable, or if he would shrug

and go to work. I wanted to know how I would feel paying for sex from someone who wasn't attracted to me. If feeling his hard warm body against mine, his cock mine to command, would compensate for his lack of interest.

And I really wanted to know what it was like to be so hot that people paid money to fuck you. I wasn't homely, but I *was* invisible—the girl who got overlooked, the girl for whom the friend zone was invented. At twenty-six, I'd long since made my peace with this. But Dalton's frequent nocturnal visits to the hotel made me aware that sexual magnetism and money were just different kinds of currency, and that I had little of either.

One hour went by and then another. Dalton was still up there. That was unusual. He rarely spent the night with anyone and worked mostly in one- or two-hour shifts.

Almost three hours after his arrival, the soft ping of the elevator sounded. He walked into the lobby looking defeated and annoyed. To my delight, he came straight for the desk.

"Bad night?" I asked.

"Horrible," he said. "I hate clients like her. They don't know what they want and no matter what you do, it's never enough."

Her. A small spurt of jealousy went through me for that woman who'd just had three naked hours with Dalton. "Nothing you can do about that, I guess."

"Well…" He hesitated and gave me a disturbed look. "Okay, I'm just going to ask. When a woman says she wants to be dominated, what the hell is she expecting?"

It was all I could do not to laugh. "Hasn't anyone requested that before?"

"Yeah, all the time. And they love it. I hold their arms down over their head, pull their hair, tell them what a dirty girl they are… I've even spanked them before." He looked defiant.

Sometimes I forgot how young he was. "Dalton, that's how

vanilla women like to be dominated. Submissive women are a different story. I'm guessing your client was a sub."

A frown creased his brow. Apparently even professional sex workers weren't always versed in BDSM. "Okay, so what do subs want?"

"Some want you to degrade them. Some want you to control them or punish them, or just bind and tease them with sensation. They're all different. But mostly they want you to take over."

"And how do you know so much about it?"

I leaned back in my chair, locked eyes with him and smiled. He got it.

"Wow." He looked away from me, embarrassed. I wondered if it made him uncomfortable to think about me sexually, his front-desk pal.

"Okay." He pushed his disheveled hair back. "So tell me what to do. I tried everything and she just laughed at me."

Poor Dalton. "There isn't a secret formula. Like I said, every-one's got different triggers."

"Nina, this is my job," he said with real anguish. "I can't be laughed at. Help me out."

"I...I can't. Seriously, it's something you have to feel."

He leaned his arms on the desk and looked in my eyes. "My whole job is about faking things I don't feel," he said pointedly.

True. But I still didn't want to propose the obvious. "You could try watching some domination porn."

"Or you could teach me." He looked hesitant.

Something fluttered deep in my gut. He had suggested it. It was his idea.

"Okay," I said. My voice was weak. I was always afraid of jinxing it when I was about to get what I wanted.

* * *

The next night I met Dalton at the hotel two hours before my shift. I'd already gotten the key for the room and taken it offline so it couldn't be assigned to a guest. Initially, he'd suggested my apartment, but the thought made me a little squirmy. I didn't know if I could transition from seeing him naked in my bed to casually greeting him at work again. And the truth was that the idea of conducting a kinky lesson upstairs in the hotel while none of my coworkers knew I was on the premises was kind of exciting. So we met at a side door and took the back elevators up to the third floor.

Oddly, he seemed more nervous than I was. I couldn't imagine why, given that he met strangers for sex for a living. Hotels were as much his workplace as mine.

He tapped my bag. "What's in there?"

"Tools." I hadn't brought anything too advanced, but I was curious how he'd react to them. "Just basic stuff."

The elevator stopped and we got out and walked down the green-and-gold-patterned corridor. Next to me, Dalton seemed even taller than I'd thought.

"So am I going to need a whole kit for this kind of job?"

"I would think the clients would provide their own toys, but you'd know that better than me." I opened the door.

The thrill of erotic anticipation flooded me as I took in the dual queen beds, oak bureau and matching table. The generic blandness and sterility seemed as always like a sanctum of anonymity, a promise that any sex here meant nothing as soon as the door closed at checkout time. It was why I loved hotel rooms. The utter lack of history and context seemed to make it possible to transform into the woman I wanted to be.

My hands were shaking. To keep him from noticing, I tossed the bag on the bed and began to unpack it. Out came the nipple clamps, the spreader bar, the paddle and the cuffs. Dalton watched with fascination. "Christ, look at all this kinky stuff."

I couldn't hold back. "Dalton, you're a pro. How can you be shocked by all this? Don't you see freaky stuff all the time?"

"Not really," he said. "Most of my clients want your basic suck and fuck. You'd be surprised how boring escorting can be."

He was right—I was surprised. "But what about your regular sex life?" I asked curiously. "What kind of sex are you into?"

Dalton looked startled, then blushed and sat on the other bed. "Nothing. I mean, just regular stuff."

It sounded like I'd found a sensitive spot. Interesting. But I didn't probe. Instead I pulled my T-shirt over my head and unsnapped my bra, letting it fall to the floor.

I sat down topless on the bed, facing him. He looked at my nipples, then quickly looked away again. It was incredible how shy he was being, unless this was an act.

I held out the clamps. "Put these on me."

"They look like they'd hurt."

"Dalton, just put them on me."

As he fumbled with the clamps, I began our first lesson. "It's a myth that BDSM is all about hard-core pain. Some people are into that, but for most of us it's about sensation and power exchange. Here, screw it a little tighter…it's okay…right, like that."

He stared at my nipples. They were flushing a darker pink now. "How does that feel?"

"It's more about how it will feel later. When you take them off, my nipples will be so sensitive you can make me come just touching them."

He laughed awkwardly and ducked his head.

"Dominate me," I ordered him.

"What?"

"Just give it your best shot. Tell me what to do, order me around."

He got to his feet. For one comical moment, he raised his index finger as if he were going to scold me. "Take off your pants."

His tone wasn't exactly masterful. I got up and stepped out of my jeans and panties, then sat back down. He loomed over me as if thinking about what to do next. "Now what?"

I suppressed a sigh. "Look, Dalton, I know you don't actually want me, but pretend that you do. Tell me to spread my legs and show you my pussy. Tell me to finger myself, or get on all fours. Grope me. Tell me you're going to do whatever you want to me because I'm just a little slut and there's nothing I can do to stop it."

The color in his face deepened and he began to laugh nervously. "I would feel ridiculous saying all that. I mean, when you say it, it sounds good but..."

Then I understood the problem. I stood up and took off the nipple clamps.

"We're doing this wrong," I told him. "A lot of people believe you have to submit before you can dominate. So I'm going to show you, okay?"

He ran a hand through his hair and laughed again. Was I imagining the relief in his voice? "Okay."

"Take off your clothes. All of them."

Now he was on familiar ground. Dalton backed up and began to pull off his shirt. He looked at the wall with this weird smile and I realized just how embarrassed he really was. I was the one whose presence had been requested tonight and he was the one who had done the requesting. He didn't know who was the client here, him or me, and the ambiguity had robbed him of his usual confidence.

His body was my idea of perfect—lean and sinewy, with a nicely sculpted chest and hard stomach. I held my breath as he pushed down his jeans. Good Christ, his cock was big: long and thick and a bit veiny, outsized in comparison to his narrow hips.

"Good boy." I tried not to let my voice betray the excitement rampaging through me. "Now stand still."

I stood up and walked a slow circle around him. I was dying to know when he'd gotten hard: when I got naked or when I began to dominate him. I supposed it didn't matter, though the first would have been a nice compliment. "Lock your hands on the back of your neck."

His long back arched as he obeyed. I ran one fingertip down his spine, then cupped his ass. He had surprisingly round cheeks given his sinewy build and—oh, yes—they were virgin pale. He'd never been spanked, not recently at least, and I suspected not ever.

My heart raced. I reminded myself to play this out properly.

I stroked his thighs. He shivered. We hadn't negotiated limits or talked about safewords; in fact, we hadn't even talked about how much sex this instruction would actually involve, but his stiff cock was dark with engorgement, his balls were tight, and a pearly web of precome gleamed in the hotel lamplight. He was aching for this. It was written in his shaking thighs and the dazed mix of hope and entreaty in his eyes.

I slid my fingers over his balls and our gazes locked.

"Don't look me in the eye." I snapped my fingers near his face. "Look at the floor."

He obeyed. What a good boy. Even so, I pushed him down on the bed and hit his thighs lightly with the crop. "Open."

Dalton didn't even wince, suggesting he might enjoy a little sting on his skin, and spread his legs like he was showing off his big cock for a photo shoot.

I ran a light fingertip over his eyelids to close them. "Some subs like to be blindfolded," I explained, "and that might be something for you to consider with your clients. It's a form of sensory deprivation and it lets them pretend you're whoever they want."

"Okay..." He sounded confused by this sudden insertion of instruction.

I scratched my fingernails down his chest. He twitched. "And if you don't know how much pain they can take, find out by doing some tests on a scale of one to ten."

"Nina." His voice was hoarse. It sounded as if he was afraid I was going to retreat into professor mode and never deliver on this physical journey we'd started.

"Yeah?"

"What do you want me to do?"

Excellent question. I cropped him once more. "What I want is for you to lie there like my obedient pet boy and shut up. You don't move, you don't talk. You just lie there like a toy and let me use you, understand?"

"Yes, Mistress."

Mistress! We hadn't even discussed how he should address me and here he was sliding into sub space on his own. I was sure now that Dalton was passionately submissive by nature, good at pleasing his clients and obeying their requests, but no doubt dreaming of a sterner hand. I wondered how often he fantasized about this: sex where he was no longer responsible for the delivery but could lie back and be delivered to.

I got to work, locking his feet into the spreader bar and cuffing his wrists over his head. My stiff nipples were hot and my cheeks were flushed, and I could feel my wetness on the top of my thighs. All of my dreams about Dalton had been explicit, but in none of them had I even dared to hope for this much.

I sat on the bed and pulled him over my knee. That pale, sumptuous ass was trembling. I lightly smacked his right cheek with the paddle and he jumped. "Oh, come on now, that was nothing," I said. "You can take more than that."

I gave him a second smack on the left and he groaned. "I— oh, my god..." He clawed at the bedspread. So this was the fire at the heart of his secret fantasies: being spanked. I kept up a steady rhythm on those firm cheeks, the slap of the paddle in rhythm with his squirming on my lap. His erection was wedged between my bare thighs and as the spanking went on, he groaned harder, struggling to rub his cock against my skin.

Much as I enjoyed it, that just wouldn't do. I pushed him onto the bed.

"Is this what you want?" His green eyes looked half wild. I rubbed his cock until he was jerking and twisting on the bedspread, straining against his bonds. Okay, we were off script at this point. I wasn't really teaching him anything so much as exploiting the situation. But Dalton was panting and pushing his cock at me like he was begging for any part of me he could get.

I straddled his narrow hips, pushed his shaft against my thigh and spanked it. "You're my little bitch, aren't you?"

"Yes, Mistress."

I squeezed him until a soft guttural noise escaped him. "You're my toy to use however I please, aren't you?"

"Yes, yes, yes."

I pulled a condom out of my bag and wrapped up his dick, stroking him up and down my wet slit. The promise of him inside me was so good that my mouth was dry and I wanted to consume every inch of him. But I eased him in slowly, bit by bit, his enormous girth stretching my pussy walls. I'd always imagined mounting him and riding my way to heaven on his cock. The reality was a little more difficult. I balanced myself on his chest so I could control the depth of penetration. When he was lodged halfway inside me, I leaned over until my nipples just barely grazed his chest.

He gave a little grunt and tried to thrust into me deeper. I remained still, making him work for access. Even bound up, he used his hips like a pro, pushing a little deeper inside me with every thrust. It felt incredible, the sensation of his muscles twisting and straining beneath me just for the privilege of experiencing my pussy.

Dalton looked half drunk with lust now, his blond hair darkened with sweat. I reached beneath me and lightly stroked my clit. A warm whirlpool was building inside me, an insistent demand to sit all the way down on his cock, but there was a specific response I wanted from him first.

"Nina, *please*. Please just fuck me."

I loved being begged. A rush of euphoria shot through me and I moved back until I was completely enveloping his cock. This was the nexus of domination for me, being craved and needed so desperately that the enslaved boy at my feet lost all pride and control. A strangled noise of gratitude escaped Dalton as my pussy surrounded every inch of him, and I began to move and twist on top of him until he was bucking desperately beneath me.

"Don't stop," he cried. "Please, don't stop…"

I might have punished a different sub for such an outburst. But I knew Dalton's plea was born out of desperation, that we weren't mistress and sub or teacher and student anymore but us, Nina and Dalton, fucking our hearts out from a need that had been there all along. I leaned over and gripped his damp blond hair in my fists like the reins of a horse, and rode him with a vengeance. Our rhythm was urgent and primal now, his enormous cock ramming me into the most delicious kind of soreness. My every nerve was drowning in fire. He struggled beneath me against the cuffs and spreader bar, a spectacle of beautiful, bound helplessness, and as he groaned again, I began coming in mindless wet shudders. Dalton let go and followed suit, hips working furiously to pump out his orgasm.

When we caught our breath, I climbed off him and looked at the clock. Time to shower and get ready for the night audit. I unlocked Dalton.

He rolled over onto his stomach, shaking out his legs and arms. He didn't speak at first and I wondered if I had pushed him too far. Finally he got up and began to dress without meeting my eyes.

"Thanks," he said. "I have to say, I would never have guessed that you were submissive."

"I'm not."

He looked confused. "You said…"

"I didn't say anything. I smiled and you assumed."

Now he gave me a wary look of suspicion, as if I had tricked him. But he nodded finally and said, "You're hard to read, Nina… I admire that about you."

I knew he meant it as a compliment. "I'm sorry I didn't give you more pointers on how to dominate your clients," I said. "I suppose this wasn't that helpful."

He avoided my eyes again. "Yeah. We should probably do it a few more times, so I can take notes or something."

He scurried out without saying good-bye. I didn't let myself watch him vanish down the corridor past all those other rooms he had been inside before. Instead I fell back on the bed, reveling in my solitude in that generic hotel room, where everything was temporary and I could be anyone, and every secret wish granted was a stepping stone to transformation.

THE FATTENING ROOM

Giselle Renarde

Jeremy was scared shitless of Nigeria, but he wasn't about to tell Nneka that.

"Say again?" his cousin Stephanie asked. Her smile was so saccharine it gave him a toothache.

Nneka wasn't all that complicated a name. Why could nobody get it on the first pass? If his fiancée were named Nina, nobody would ask for repetition.

"Neh-nee-kah." She pronounced her name slowly for Steph, over-enunciating every syllable. That made Jeremy smile. Nneka would never roll over for anyone.

Cousin Stephanie clung to her wineglass like a lifeline. "And you're from Nairobi?"

Everybody else at this family gathering was entirely nonchalant about him marrying an African woman. Why did Steph have to act like a dink?

"She's from Nigeria," Jeremy corrected.

Stephanie nodded a few times then cocked her head. "And that's in Kenya?"

"No, Nairobi is in Kenya," Nneka said. "Nigeria is a country."

"Are you from the North or the South?"

Jeremy swung around to find Uncle Stu standing behind him. He hadn't realized anyone was listening in on their conversation, but at least his uncle was a little more worldly than his darling daughter.

Nneka looked at Uncle Stu with what seemed like a combination of apprehension and amusement. "From the South."

Uncle Stu tapped the base of his scotch glass with his middle finger. "Then your people would be Yoruba or...Ibo?"

Nneka seemed blown away by his knowledge of her home country. "Yeah, Ibo."

"Wow, Daddy," Stephanie gushed. "How did you know?"

At thirty-five, she really was too old to call her father "Daddy."

"Oh, it was all in the news during the Biafran War—not that any of you kids are old enough to remember those days. But I bet your parents have told you a great deal about it, Nneka."

She smiled widely when he pronounced her name right. "My grandparents, too. I've been living here since I was four years old, but every time my brother and I go back home, my grandmother tells me all about the old days."

Cousin Steph walked away, gravitating to a more entertaining conversation as Jeremy and his uncle shifted across the room. They sat in the wingchairs by the window like spectators while Nneka stood before them, speaking excitedly of Nigeria.

For as long as Jeremy had known Nneka, he'd never thought of her as a girl from another country, a girl who was any less Canadian than himself. She'd never spoken with an accent, at least not one that he could perceive. Now, the more Nneka talked about the place of her birth, sharing her grandmother's stories, the more her speech patterns changed. None of the usual concise, clipped pronunciations. Everything expanded. Phrases grew fat in her mouth. Her manner of discourse became slow, swaying the way her hips did when they walked along the beach. She told the old tales.

Nneka was a brainiac. Nneka was an academic. As Jeremy listened to his normally reserved fiancée talking like a tribal storyteller, he felt uncomfortable. He didn't want to feel that way, but he kept thinking how she'd done such a good job of impressing his family so far. Why ruin it with stories from the African fire pit? God, he didn't want to get married in Nigeria. He didn't want to go anywhere near Nigeria.

All the way home, Jeremy tried to formulate the perfect question, but everything he came up with sounded either judgmental or downright ignorant. "You seemed to enjoy telling my Uncle Stu all your grandmother's stories," he finally said when they arrived back at the condo.

"Not all of them," she replied, obviously missing the point.

"I just meant…" Jeremy opened the refrigerator door by rote. He stared inside. "I've never heard you talk like that before."

"Meaning what?" Nneka was taking off her jewelry. He could hear the signature clink of gold hitting the ceramic dish in the bedroom.

"Meaning…" Christ, he didn't know what he was trying to say. He was going to end up in the doghouse if he went too far down this road. "Just…I've never heard you speak with an accent. It was…strange."

There was a long stretch of silence from the bedroom. A long stretch. Jeremy grabbed the bottle of Perrier on the door, wanting to drink it all down, but he didn't dare budge until he knew what he was in for. Was she pissed? She must be pissed.

And then, thank god, Nneka laughed. It wasn't even her

"You're a bastard" cackle—it was genuine "I'm amused" laughter. Sauntering into the hallway, Nneka sang, "Who's afraid of the big black girl?"

Jeremy nearly dropped the Perrier when he realized she'd stripped down to her slip. He knew she wore it as a slimming garment, but he didn't give a fuck what purpose it served. To him, that skin-tight black underdress spelled instant erection. When his gaze landed in her ample cleavage, he couldn't remember what the hell they'd been talking about.

"You cooling yourself down in the fridge, there?" Nneka laughed at him, but he didn't care. She'd left on those strappy black sandals he loved so much. God, he'd probably come before he got his pants off.

"I'm...you...wow..."

Nneka sauntered into the living room, snapping on the reading lamp in the corner. "I'll take that as a compliment, shall I?" She stood in front of their floor-to-ceiling window like an exhibitionist, and Jeremy was jealous of everyone down at street level. Those lucky bastards could see her from behind.

Setting the Perrier bottle on the counter, Jeremy tripped over his feet to get close to her. "I'm gonna fuck you so hard..."

"Sit." She pointed to the sofa, and he followed her instruction without reflection. Her face, illuminated by the soft yellow glow of the table lamp, seemed both joyful and stern. He wasn't sure just yet if he was going to get it or if he was going to *get* it. "Did I ever tell you about the fattening room?"

"Fattening room?" Jeremy was stupid with arousal. He shook his head. He didn't care. He just wanted to shove his face between her big thighs and take in the scent of her hot cunt. He wanted to eat her pussy until she was so turned on she trapped him there between her legs. When the fat of her thighs blocked all sound from his ears, he could swear he heard the voice of God.

Nneka came close and stood between his open legs. She fondled the back of his neck with both hands as he looked past her big boobs and into her dark eyes. When he grabbed her ass, she backed away, wagging her finger at him like he'd been a naughty, naughty boy. She reached for the stereo and danced in place to the world music that came through the speakers. This was all strange, so unlike the Nneka he knew, but he didn't care anymore. He was intrigued and enamored, and horny as hell!

"In my country, the men, they like their women fat." Nneka's words were heavy and slow, like thick syrup. She pronounced *the* like *dee, they* like *dey*. She was channeling her grandmother again, and this time Jeremy wasn't afraid of the big black girl. In every sense possible, he wanted her.

"Fat…" Jeremy reached for her hands, but she waggled both index fingers at him this time. No, no, no. She danced without lifting her feet from the carpet.

"When my grandmother was a girl, she was promised to a man in the town. Before the ceremony take place, her mother put her in the fattening room. The women, they lock her up inside, and for six month they fatten her up for the man. Her husband want his wife fat."

"Fat…" The word rumbled in Jeremy's belly like a hunger, and then rumbled lower like a different kind of hunger.

"For six month, the women feed her meat, feed her fat. She eat cassava, plantain, *fufu, banga* soup. They feed her one meal, and when she finish, they feed her the next. One food after another after another, and she wear the bones from the meat around her big belly. She get fat, my lover. She get big and fat all over."

Jeremy felt a timidity come over him as Nneka approached, closer and closer, moving and gyrating right in front of him. It was like getting a lap dance from another man's wife. His fiancée was possessed…or released? When he reached for her this time, she didn't shoo his hands away. He ran his fingers down the outsides of her thighs and back up again. God, she was beautiful. He tore down the top of her slip, pressing his eager face between her big breasts as they toppled out of those sturdy cups.

Nneka gasped when he sucked her nipples. She pressed his head flush to her tits and continued her grandmother's story: "On ceremony day, the women rub her body with camwood and *uli* to make her skin dark and smooth. They dress her in wraps of every color, and they take her to meet her husband. Everybody so happy when they see how fat she get, they all sing and they dance her round the market. And her husband, he love her fat. He take her home and make love to her fat."

Jeremy couldn't stand any more. Her voice, that raspy velvet she'd put on to tell this story, made his head spin. He was too dizzy to stand, too giddy to do anything but suck her tits and fondle her ass. "Fat," he heard himself saying as he squeezed her flesh with both hands. "We gotta make you fat, woman. You're getting married in three months."

"Put me in the fattening room?" Nneka's voice was still not her own, but Jeremy didn't care. He tugged the clinging fabric down her body, pulling it hard past the roundness of her belly, yanking it over her ass, pushing it to the floor.

He was surprised to find in himself the fortitude not only to stand, but to press his fiancée down on the couch. Racing to the kitchen, he caught sight of the Perrier bottle he'd left on the counter. Little good that would do him now. He opened up the freezer and pulled out the tub of chocolate ice cream. He scooped it into a big bowl and added every topping he could find: whipped marshmallow, chocolate sauce, caramel, and at least six cherries on top.

"Here," he said, handing her the huge bowl of ice cream.

He didn't know what he was saying anymore. He'd totally lost control. "This man wants his woman fat."

She didn't mention the gown she'd have to squeeze into for the ceremony. Maybe she'd decided to go with traditional Ibo wedding apparel. Before tonight, Jeremy would have objected— in fact, before tonight he had objected. Not anymore. Now he wanted what she wanted, and he wanted the fullness of her. Nneka was more than just a nice buttoned-down Canadian girl; she was her grandmother's granddaughter, too. There was so much inside of her, so much she must have suppressed to fit in in this country—to fit in with him, even. He felt a little ashamed of himself for keeping her down all this time. But all that was going to change.

Her body was so big, so full, and Jeremy sat beside her as she savored her dessert. His hands had minds of their own— they took off across the expanse of her thighs, kneading that supple flesh. Thighs, belly...oh, so much belly...wide hips, big tits. She was so beautiful, so dark, so wonderfully edible. Her skin gleamed with cocoa butter. She smelled good enough to eat, and Jeremy didn't even try to resist.

"Eat," Jeremy instructed. She was just sitting there watching him, highly amused. "Eat and get fat, woman."

Nneka leaned back like an odalisque against the side arm of the sofa. She raised an eyebrow—he'd never called her "woman" before tonight—but scooped melting ice cream onto her spoon. After dunking it in marshmallow and a deep well of fudge and caramel, she raised it up to her lips. When she paused, he prayed it would drop. Jeremy wanted to watch that spoonful drizzle down her breast. Rubbing her thighs up and down, building hot friction, he silently begged the ice cream to fall off the spoon. It didn't. Nneka shuttled it into her mouth, and it emerged clean as a whistle. She licked hot fudge from her full lips, and Jeremy wanted that tongue, that mouth. He wanted everything, and he didn't know why.

Like a child, Jeremy stole the ice-cream dish back from his fiancée.

"Give it," she commanded, steeling her gaze. She didn't even reach for it.

"You want it?" he asked. He wasn't sure what he was getting himself into, here. How would she react when he scooped up a spoonful of chocolate ice cream and hot fudge, and drizzled it down the length of her belly? What would she do when he coated her tits in marshmallow and her thighs in caramel?

Nneka gasped when the cold met her flesh, but she laughed at everything else. "My lover want to fatten himself up?"

Jeremy returned a smile as he fell to his knees on the floor beside the couch. "I could stand to put on a few pounds."

When he handed her the ice-cream bowl, she purred like Eartha Kitt. "I eat ice cream, you eat me?"

"That's the idea," Jeremy replied before diving at her left thigh. The caramel spread across her flesh was heavy and sweet, and he licked it like an animal, working his way up for chocolate from her belly and marshmallow from her breast. Everything was too saccharine, but the combination made it all bearable. He could taste the salt of Nneka's flesh as he licked her, and the cocoa butter that made her skin gleam.

The clink of the spoon against the glass bowl drew Jeremy's gaze upward, and he savored the image of Nneka naked, eyes closed, lost in the bliss of a chocolate orgasm. She made sounds, lots of sounds, as he licked her and she ate: "Mmmm… ohhhhhh…yesssss…" Her face was so beautiful like that, like it was both pained and thoroughly relaxed. She looked like she'd risen to another plane of existence.

"Get fat," Jeremy encouraged. He could play this game now.

He understood. "This man wants his woman fat."

"I am fat," Nneka cooed, drizzling chocolate sauce across her breasts for him to lick. "But I will get fatter."

He sucked her mammoth tits through clouds of marshmallow. His chin, his nose, his cheeks were all sticky with sauces. The sugar made his head buzz—or was that the arousal? Was that the big, black, beautiful woman lying naked on the couch? Her ecstasy ran through him as he ducked between her thighs, opening them as wide as he could, pressing them apart. Her pussy glistened at the apex, and the very sight of those shimmering pink folds made him growl. She opened for him, beckoning his tongue more effectively even than the syrups drizzled the length of her flesh.

Nneka was a mess of sauces now, all sticky and sweet, but nothing could possibly tempt him more than the candy flesh dripping nectar down, down, down until it disappeared from sight. She scooped ice cream into her mouth, moaning after every spoonful. He needed her now. He needed to taste that inner part of the woman he would soon wed, and he nuzzled her pussy, rubbing his lips against her erect clit. She was so wet, so damnably wet, and he opened his mouth to consume her. He couldn't resist.

When he licked her that first time, with his tongue still sweet from syrup, she jumped. Her hips rose up from the couch and Jeremy slipped his hands beneath the roundness of her ass. Her flesh melted in his grasp, and when he squeezed, she moaned.

Gazing down from her armrest perch, from behind a forest of flesh and a bowl of ice cream, she said, "Eat me, lover."

Had he been waiting for her to ask? Maybe he had, because now, with her permission, her solicitation even, he plunged his face between her thighs and ate, ate, ate. He licked Nneka's wet pussy, slurping her nectar like a man with unquenchable thirst.

The taste of her was nothing like the sweet sauces, nothing like chocolate—it was heavy, musky and far superior to any ice cream he'd ever tasted.

"Eat me!" she cried, pressing his head flush to her cunt with one strong hand. He could feel the chill of her metal spoon against his neck, just above his shirt collar. She was entirely naked, and he was entirely dressed.

Harder, he went at her harder, sucking her erect clit into his mouth, devouring her fat pussy lips. He took in everything he could and sucked that supple flesh like a cock, up and down, thrusting his face against her pelvis. His forehead landed in the cushion of her belly, and he could feel the chocolate sauce in his hair now. Did this make him her candy man, the fact that he was covered in syrups? What the hell was a candy man, anyway? Was it like a sugar daddy? Because he definitely wasn't that, not to Nneka. He was a partner in every sense. He was the man at her side—not in front of her, not behind her, but right there beside her. And he wasn't going anywhere.

Nneka cried out now. Even when she trapped his head between her thighs, he could still hear her shrieks and moans. If their neighbors were listening in, they'd think he was killing her. Nneka never could put a lid on it in bed. Or on the couch.

Digging his fingers into the flesh of her ass, Jeremy ate her like crazy. His mobility was limited by her thighs, but that didn't stop him sucking her clit and pussy lips. Everything was wet, so wet and sticky and sweet and musky.

He could feel her body trembling now. She crossed her legs over his back, bringing him closer, trapping him between her thighs—like he'd ever try to escape! Her cries were muffled vibrations running through her body, transferred from the flesh of her thighs to his ears. He experienced her pleasure directly. He felt it in her as she came. When he listened, he listened with his whole self. He trembled with her, sweating through his shirt, shuddering with highest bliss, the most thorough and life-altering joy.

These moments...ah, these moments...

Nneka quieted. Her body's motion quelled. What was her flesh singing now? Humming more like, chants to the gods, like an afterthought of love. Jeremy pressed his cheek against her thigh, even after her body released him. She was messy, he was messy, and they laughed at each other, so endearingly his heart felt too big for his chest.

After many soft moments, he opened his mouth to speak. No sound came out, but he tried again. "I'm sorry I've been so negative about the wedding."

Her voice was her own, or at least it was the voice he recognized as hers. "How about I spend the next three months in the fattening room? You won't be able to resist me."

"I can't resist you now." He kissed her pussy and she shuddered, then ran her fingers through his hair. He grabbed her hand, bringing it to his lips and kissing her knuckles. "All I care is that we're doing what's important to you. I guess I didn't understand before, but...I do now."

"You do?"

He sucked her sweet fingertips and nodded slowly. "I do."

She met him with a dulcet gaze before pulling him to her mouth. Her tongue writhed against his, sweet with chocolate and caramel. Even through all that sugar, the taste of her pussy remained strongest of all. He'd go to Nigeria to be married before Nneka's family, because Nneka meant the world to him, and her faraway kin meant the world to her.

For this woman, he'd go anywhere.

ABOUT THE AUTHORS

VALERIE ALEXANDER lives in Arizona. Her work has been previously published in *Best of Best Women's Erotica, Best Bondage Erotica* and other anthologies.

JANINE ASHBLESS is the author of five Black Lace erotica books of paranormal and fantasy erotica. Her short stories have been published by Cleis Press in the anthologies *I Is for Indecent; Playing with Fire; Frenzy; Best Women's Erotica 2009;* and *Best Bondage Erotica 2011.* She blogs at janineashbless. blogspot.com.

MARY BORSELLINO writes short erotica, pop culture analysis and punk young adult novels. She hates grape-flavored latex. Her website is maryborsellino.com.

RACHEL KRAMER BUSSEL (rachelkramerbussel.com) is a writer, editor, blogger and event organizer. She's edited more than forty anthologies, including *Spanked; Bottoms Up; Please, Sir;*

Please, Ma'am; and *Best Bondage Erotica 2011* and *2012*. She is senior editor at *Penthouse Variations*, sex columnist for *SexIs* magazine and covers sex, dating, books and pop culture widely.

ELIZABETH COLDWELL lives and writes in London. Her spanking-themed stories have appeared in anthologies including *Spanked*, *Bottoms Up* and *Naughty Spanking 2* and *3*. She can be found at The (Really) Naughty Corner, elizabethcoldwell. wordpress.com.

LUCY FELTHOUSE (lucyfelthouse.co.uk) is a graduate of the University of Derby, where she studied creative writing. During her first year, she was dared to write an erotic story—so she did. It went down a storm and she's never looked back. Lucy is also the editor of *Uniform Behavior, Seducing the Myth, Smut by the Sea* and *Smut in the City*.

MIMI KESSEL (mimikessel.com) started writing erotica for herself until she realized the seductive possibilities. Then she thought, why not go pro? She is a marathon bather who has only dropped a book into a bathtub once in her entire life.

KRISSY KNEEN is the author of *Affection: An Erotic Memoir* and *Triptych: An Erotic Adventure*. She has been shortlisted for the Australian Book Industry Awards (Biography) and the Queensland Premier's Literary Awards (Nonfiction). Her short work has been published in various literary magazines including *Griffith REVIEW* and Nerve.com.

SERAFINE LAVEAUX was born in Eden Isle, Louisiana and briefly attended the University of New Orleans, but left to marry her current husband. At his encouragement, she began writing erotica at the age of twenty-two. She and her husband Roger live just outside New Orleans with their five dogs and a cat.

JENNY LYN (authorjennylyn.com) is a published erotic romance and erotica writer who lives in a swampy corner of Florida with her family. She loves the heat, both climate-wise and otherwise. The mosquitoes and hurricanes...not so much.

ANNA MEADOWS is a part-time executive assistant, part-time lesbian housewife. Her work appears in six Cleis Press anthologies, including *Steamlust: Steampunk Erotic Romance* and *Girls Who Bite: Lesbian Vampire Erotica*. She lives and writes in Northern California.

ANIKA RAY's writing previously appeared in *Sweet Confessions,* edited by Violet Blue, as well as elsewhere. When not writing, she likes to travel, read and surf.

GISELLE RENARDE is a queer Canadian, contributor to many anthologies and author of dozens of electronic and print books, including *Anonymous, Nanny State, Audrey & Lawrence, Ondine, Secret Confessions* and *The Red Satin Collection*. Giselle's book *My Mistress' Thighs: Erotic Transgender Fiction and Poetry* received an Honorable Mention in the 2011 Rainbow Awards.

CHARLOTTE STEIN has published many stories in various anthologies, including *Fairy Tale Lust*. Her own collection of shorts was named one of the best erotic romances of 2009 by Michelle Buonfiglio. She also has novellas out with Ellora's Cave, Total-E-Bound and Xcite, and you can contact her here: themightycharlottestein.blogspot.com.

ELIANI TORRES is a freelance copy editor by trade: "I live and write in southern Vermont, where I am at work on a rural horror novel set in the hollows and hill towns of the Green Mountains. My fiction has appeared in *Strange Horizons, Whatever* and *Farthing.*"

ALYSSA TURNER's writings address a woman's desire to really have it all—including the things she's not supposed to want. She writes for Xcite Books and Etopia Press, with several full-length erotic romance epublications currently available. Her debut publication was a short in *Best Women's Erotica 2011.*

Called a "Trollop with a Laptop," a "Literary Siren," and "The Mistress of Literary Erotica," **ALISON TYLER** lives to be naughty. She is the editor of more than fifty erotic anthologies, including thirty-five for Cleis Press, most recently *Morning, Noon and Night* and *Sudden Sex.* Please visit alisontyler.blogspot.com.

ROSALIA ZIZZO is a hot-blooded Sicilian whose work has appeared on several online sites and in various publications, including anthologies like *Nice Girls Naughty Sex, Forbidden Desires II, Best Women's Erotica 2012* and *Stretched.* Smiling in her wheelchair, she lets you see that multiple sclerosis only makes her more fiercely independent.

VIOLET BLUE (tinynibbles.com, @violetblue) is an award-winning author and editor, CNET reporter, CBSi/ZDNet blogger and columnist, a high-profile tech personality and one of *Wired*'s Faces of Innovation. She is regarded as the foremost expert in the field of sex and technology, a sex-positive mainstream media pundit (*MacLife,* CNN, "The Oprah Winfrey Show") and is interviewed, quoted and featured in outlets ranging from ABC News to the *Wall Street Journal.*

Blue was the notorious sex columnist for the *San Francisco Chronicle.* She has been at the center of many Internet scandals, including Google's "nymwars" and Libya's web domain censorship and seizures—*Forbes* calls her "omnipresent on the web" and named her a Forbes Web Celeb. She headlines and keynotes at global technology conferences including ETech, LeWeb, SXSW: Interactive and two Google Tech Talks at Google, Inc. and received a standing ovation at Seattle's Gnomedex.

The *London Times* named Violet Blue "one of the 40 bloggers who really count."

More Women's Erotica from Violet Blue

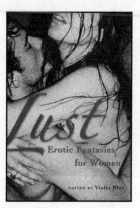

Best Erotica Series

"Gets racier every year."—*San Francisco Bay Guardian*

**Buy 4 books,
Get 1 *FREE****

Best Women's Erotica 2012
Edited by Violet Blue
ISBN 978-1-57344-755-3 $15.95

Best Women's Erotica 2011
Edited by Violet Blue
ISBN 978-1-57344-423-1 $15.95

Best Women's Erotica 2010
Edited by Violet Blue
ISBN 978-1-57344-373-9 $15.95

Best Bondage Erotica 2012
Edited by Rachel Kramer Bussel
ISBN 978-1-57344-754-6 $15.95

Best Bondage Erotica 2011
Edited by Rachel Kramer Bussel
ISBN 978-1-57344-426-2 $15.95

Best Fetish Erotica
Edited by Cara Bruce
ISBN 978-1-57344-355-5 $15.95

Best Lesbian Erotica 2012
Edited by Kathleen Warnock. Selected and
introduced by Sinclair Sexsmith.
ISBN 978-1-57344-752-2 $15.95

Best Lesbian Erotica 2011
Edited by Kathleen Warnock.
Selected and introduced by Lea DeLaria.
ISBN 978-1-57344-425-5 $15.95

Best Lesbian Erotica 2010
Edited by Kathleen Warnock.
Selected and introduced by BETTY.
ISBN 978-1-57344-375-3 $15.95

Best Gay Erotica 2012
Edited by Richard Labonté. Selected and
introduced by Larry Duplechan.
ISBN 978-1-57344-753-9, $15.95

Best Gay Erotica 2011
Edited by Richard Labonté.
Selected and introduced by Kevin Killian.
ISBN 978-1-57344-424-8 $15.95

Best Gay Erotica 2010
Edited by Richard Labonté. Selected and
introduced by Blair Mastbaum.
ISBN 978-1-57344-374-6 $15.95

In Sleeping Beauty's Bed
Erotic Fairy Tales
By Mitzi Szereto
ISBN 978-1-57344-367-8 $16.95

Can't Help the Way That I Feel
Sultry Stories of African American Love
Edited by Lori Bryant-Woolridge
ISBN 978-1-57344-386-9 $14.95

Making the Hook-Up
Edgy Sex with Soul
Edited by Cole Riley
ISBN 978-1-57344-3838 $14.95

* Free book of equal or lesser value. Shipping and applicable sales tax extra.
Cleis Press • (800) 780-2279 • orders@cleispress.com
www.cleispress.com

Ordering is easy! Call us toll free or fax us to place your MC/VISA order.
You can also mail the order form below with payment to:
Cleis Press, 2246 Sixth St., Berkeley, CA 94710.

ORDER FORM

QTY	TITLE	PRICE
___	_____	___
___	_____	___
___	_____	___
___	_____	___
___	_____	___
___	_____	___
___	_____	___
___	_____	___

	SUBTOTAL	___
	SHIPPING	___
	SALES TAX	___
	TOTAL	___

Add $3.95 postage/handling for the first book ordered and $1.00 for each additional book. Outside North America, please contact us for shipping rates. California residents add 8.75% sales tax. Payment in U.S. dollars only.

* Free book of equal or lesser value. Shipping and applicable sales tax extra.

Cleis Press • Phone: (800) 780-2279 • Fax: (510) 845-8001
orders@cleispress.com • www.cleispress.com
You'll find more great books on our website

Follow us on Twitter @cleispress • Friend/fan us on Facebook